One part sizzle, two parts seduction...

"You're beautiful," Johnny murmured.

And Natalie was. Her neck was long, her shoulders elegant and her breasts high and firm.

She reached for his shirt and he helped her tug it off, then pulled her close again, enjoying the feel of her bare skin against his.

When she leaned forward and connected a line of soft kisses from one side of his chest to the other, she almost undid him. He pushed her back on the bed, toppling her so she fell laughing onto the mattress.

He needed to distract himself. Other men might recite sports stats or set themselves math problems. Johnny tested himself on obscure drink recipes.

When he kissed her mouth, he mentally prepared a pink lady. Not a drink requested too often, but Natalie's pink-tipped nipples against her white skin made the cocktail pop into his head. He leaned over to nuzzle her breasts and she gasped, her back rising off the bed.

His ___ ___ was in her sighed "Oh, yes."

If ___ ___ ___ BRARY ___ his,
h___

Available in May 2010
from Mills & Boon® Blaze®

UNDER THE INFLUENCE

BY
NANCY WARREN

⊚™ MILLS & BOON®

First published in Great Britain 2010
Harlequin Mills & Boon Limited,
Eton House, 18-24 Paradise Road, Richmond, Surrey TW9 1SR

© Nancy Warren 2009

ISBN: 978 0 263 88132 5

14-0510

Harlequin Mills & Boon policy is to use papers that are natural, renewable
and recyclable products and made from wood grown in sustainable forests.
The logging and manufacturing processes conform to the legal environmental
regulations of the country of origin.

Printed and bound in Spain
by Litografía Rosés S.A., Barcelona

USA TODAY bestselling author **Nancy Warren** lives in the Pacific Northwest where her hobbies include walking her border collie in the rain, antiques and mixing martinis. She's the author of more than thirty novels and novellas and has won numerous awards. Visit her at www.nancywarren.net.

This is for Kathleen (again),
BAM (you know who you are!),
the wonderful people I met in Tofino
and of course Johnny,
without whom this book would
never have been written.
Bottoms up!

1

Screaming Orgasm

1 oz white crème de cacao
1 oz Amaretto almond liqueur
1 oz triple sec
1 oz vodka
2 oz light cream

Serves two.

NATALIE FANSHAW did something that night she'd never done in her twenty-nine years on earth. She walked into a bar alone.

She hovered in the doorway of the Driftwood Bar and Grill in Orca Bay, California, not sure whether to move forward or turn around and head back to her hotel room. It wasn't that she was desperate for a drink, it was more that she couldn't sit at the too-small desk in her hotel room and look at those spreadsheets for one more minute without going crazy.

The Driftwood was a popular cocktails and dinner destination. They specialized in fresh seafood, like mussels served in buckets more ways than Natalie could have imagined, and seared mahimahi with a Thai curry glaze.

The hostess approached her with a menu, her eyebrows raised. Shaking her head at both the hostess and her own timidity, Nat pulled her shoulders back and walked with purpose. Up to the gray granite bar. There were a dozen or so stools in brushed metal with black leather seats. A young couple had their stools pushed so close together they touched from knee to thigh.

Natalie chose a seat at the other end and hiked herself up onto it.

She placed her purse on the empty stool beside her in a clear Keep Away signal, then glanced around. She'd never been here before, but she knew the place by reputation. She was surprised how busy it was for a Wednesday night. Almost every table was taken, mostly by couples. These looked like romantic rather than business transactions—unlike most of her dinners out. The decor of the room was upscale casual, with a beach theme that would have looked a lot better without all the pink-and-red stuff hanging from the ceiling. And what was with the corny, oversize papier-mâché hearts wafting around like a cardiologist's nightmare?

"Help you?"

Even as the low voice spoke to her, a terrible thought struck her. "Oh, no," she said, her gaze still transfixed by those swinging hearts. "Please tell me it's not Valentine's Day?"

She glanced up at the bartender who'd spoken, and looked into the bluest eyes she had ever seen. And they were twinkling at her as though the gorgeous guy with the disheveled hair and the deeply tanned face was laughing at her without involving his mouth. "Okay," he said, "I won't tell you."

Grabbing her purse, she pulled out her BlackBerry. How had she not noticed the significance of the date? February 14. "My secretary should have reminded me," she complained bitterly.

"Somebody you forgot to send flowers to?"

She shook her head. "No. But I would have been more careful." She glanced around once more, now seeing the obvious. The twosomes holding hands, the low-voiced conversations that were all versions of "I love you," "No, *I* love *you*." Of all the nights in all the cities she'd traveled to, she had to pick this one to brave a bar alone. "I am the only singleton trapped in the Love Shack."

The bartender laughed. Low and sexy. His shirt was open at the collar. If it was hers she'd have ironed it into crisp perfection, but she had to admit the rumpled cotton looked good on him, maybe because it went with his mussed hair and aura of relaxed untidiness, as if he'd just rolled out of bed. "You're not the only one."

She glanced up, inquiring.

"I'm stuck here, too."

Was he telling her he was single, also? She was so out of touch with the whole male-female thing that she wasn't sure that's what he meant. Maybe he was simply complaining that he had to work when there was some hot chick still in his bed.

She wasn't about to ask.

"Well, since we're both here, what can I get you?"

"Oh." She looked at the rows of bottles lined up against the mirrored wall behind him. As exotic as a jewelry store, the wall winked at her. Bottles glowed with blue, pink and red. An entire row was devoted to Scotch whisky, some of which she knew was much older than she.

Then she ordered what she always ordered. "A glass of white wine, please."

She had her second shock of the night.

The bartender shook his head.

"You don't carry white wine?"

"Sure we do. But white wine is not for you. Not tonight."

Both intrigued and mildly annoyed—since Natalie was a woman who always knew her own mind, was famous in fact for her decision making—she said, "And what do you have in mind for me? Tonight?"

The moment the words left her lips she wished she could suck them back as fast as the couple down the other end of the bar were tossing back their martinis. Her words sounded low, sexy, like a come-on. The last thing she'd intended. She shifted uncomfortably on her seat. One quick drink and she was out of hearts-and-chocolates land.

The man behind the bar seemed not to notice her discomfort. He regarded her from those eyes that reminded her of the ocean and said, "Have you ever had a Blue Crush?"

Lord, she was having one now, looking into those blue, blue eyes and feeling her pulse speed up a little bit. She knew she was overtired, but still, it was quite a reaction she was having to a man she could not have less in common with.

"I've had Orange Crush," she said, "when I was a kid."

He grinned at her, even white teeth that could eat her all up. "Trust me, this one's a lot more fun."

And she thought, *What the hell? Here I am on Valentine's Day, with no Valentine, I might at least try a new drink.*

"Okay," she said. "I'll trust you."

"You won't be sorry."

Why did she find that so hard to believe?

"Right now," a twangy female voice suddenly said, coming from Natalie's left, "I need two Screaming Orgasms, one Sex on the Beach and a Roll Between the Sheets."

"You and me both," Natalie said. She didn't realize she'd spoken aloud until the woman gave a bray of laughter that was altogether bigger than her small frame could hold.

"It's Valentine's Day," the tiny waitress explained in a confidential tone. "They think if they order the raunchy drinks, they'll get laid."

"Does it work?"

The woman flipped her red-gold ponytail over her shoulder when she jerked her head toward the restaurant. "See for yourself."

Natalie looked around, and felt suddenly as though she were behind a velvet rope on the outside of one of those exclusive A-list parties one read about. And the biggest bouncer in the world was keeping her on the wrong side of the barrier.

On the other side were couples. She was no expert on mating rituals, but she could sense from the way they leaned toward each other, shared food and sipped each other's drinks that these men and women weren't going home to calculators and spreadsheets for company.

Sex was in the air as decidedly as the aroma of fresh seafood and garlic butter.

One young man had his shoe off and was tracing the inner thigh of his date with his stockinged foot, not at all shy about the fact that anyone glancing his way would see what he was up to. Of course, most of the dinner guests were too interested in their own dates to glance anywhere else. One woman gave the man across the tiny table from her a bite of her chocolate fondue, and when a sensuously rich dribble of chocolate hit his chin, they both ignored his napkin. She gave a tiny smile, leaned close, breasts thrusting forward from a skimpy top, the tip of her pink tongue showing, and licked the chocolate off.

Thoroughly.

"Oh, my," Natalie said, her hand going to her chest. Not that she was a prude, but there was a lot of raw sexual energy in the room. It got to a person.

"Don't worry," the bartender said, "we've got plenty of fire extinguishers. If the heat gets out of hand, we blast them."

"Oh, Johnny," the cocktail waitress said, with the lazy affection perfected by Southern women. She rolled her eyes, collecting her drinks on a round tray and departed.

"Johnny?" Natalie stared at the man in front of her. Of course he had no name badge. It wasn't that sort of place. But in the short time she'd been in town she'd discovered he was locally famous. With women. "You're Hot Johnny?"

2

Blue Crush

1 oz blue curaçao
1 oz Cointreau
1 oz vodka
1 oz Malibu rum
Crushed ice
Orange twist for garnish

JOHNNY LAUGHED. He couldn't help it. He'd never seen anyone give away her inner thoughts so easily as the blushing woman sitting staring at him did.

How could anyone so uptight, business suited and restrained be so much fun?

"People usually don't call me that to my face."

Of course he'd heard his nickname; he'd lived in Orca Bay for fifteen years. The nickname wasn't something he'd asked for. But Johnny had learned a long time ago that when things were good you shouldn't fight them. Women liked him. He figured it was an accident of Fate. And he'd love to meet Fate someday and shake him by the hand and buy him a drink to say thanks.

Truth was, Johnny liked women, too. Genuinely

liked their different styles and shapes and colors. Some men might write off the single woman who climbed onto a bar stool carrying a briefcase on Valentine's Day, but Johnny didn't. He liked her contrasts. Her conservative suit and the comments that escaped her mouth seemingly by accident. Her neat hairstyle and the kinky waves that suggested wildness. Her first choice, white wine, so predictable but look how quickly she'd been willing to try something new.

Definitely, there were interesting depths beneath the surface of this woman.

"I'm sorry," she said, flustered. "I didn't mean to be rude, but I heard some women talking about you." Suddenly, she blushed scarlet and he had to wonder what she'd overheard.

Hell, tonight would be a long one. Everybody seemed to be part of a couple except for him and this woman who hadn't even realized it was Valentine's Day. So he asked her. "What did you hear?"

"I can't remember."

"Shouldn't lie on Valentine's Day. It's bad luck."

She glanced at her BlackBerry as though hoping it would ring, or beep or something. But it remained as silent as he did, waiting for her answer.

"It might have been something about kissing."

Now he truly was intrigued. Who gossiped about kissing? "What about it?"

"It was just idle chitchat, you know the way women go on. I overheard these two talking. Accidentally, you know. I was in a restaurant, having a quick breakfast and reading the paper. The woman mentioned Hot Johnny and she got to kissing one time and she almost—" the blush deepened "—you know…" Now she waved in the general direction of the main dining room, "Like the drink."

He was wondering why this woman spent so much time in restaurants alone, and could picture her and her newspaper and the way her eyes must have widened when she got sex talk along with her morning coffee. "What drink?"

"The Screaming Orgasm." She whispered the words.

"Are you saying she almost came from kissing me?" How cool was that?

"No. *She* said that. This woman. Who called you Hot Johnny, and then the other woman said…well, anyway. That's how I heard of you."

"What did she look like? The woman who almost, you know…"

"I don't know, I didn't really see her. Blond, I think."

"Huh." In California, that really narrowed it down. Not that the woman's identity mattered. Didn't sound like they'd ever gone beyond mouth action. Whatever.

His new customer was certainly making his night more interesting, he thought, as he mixed the Blue Crush. He barely thought about his actions as he poured blue curaçao, rum, vodka and the other ingredients into a shaker, gave the whole a thorough blending and strained the blue concoction into a martini glass.

He reached for a twist of orange peel, knowing she was watching his every move, and added an extra twist, giving the shape a sensual sinuousness as it looped around the edge of the glass the way a stripper might twine herself around a pole.

"Thank you." She eyed it for a moment, as though

regretting her rash departure from white wine, then sipped slowly.

He watched her, enjoying the way her eyes widened slightly at the taste, the way she licked her lips consciously, a tiny frown pulling her brows together.

She stayed like that for a moment, almost Zen-like in her perfect stillness, as though every part of her were involved in tasting and evaluating her drink.

"Well?" he finally asked.

"It's good," she said, delivering the verdict, then taking another tiny sip. "I thought it might be too sweet since it's named after a soft drink."

"It's not. The drink's named after a surfing wave. The kind that knocks you on your ass."

"Oh." She glanced with trepidation at the drink. "You mean?"

"One won't do it. Don't worry."

"Oh, good, because I still have work to do tonight."

He was about to ask, but Suzanne, the head waitress, marched up to the bar with a list of orders.

She was on her way again immediately. Efficiency on legs.

While he worked, he said, "So, tell me how come you're here alone on Valentine's Day?"

She regarded him with great seriousness. "Isn't that sort of personal?"

Deftly adding a couple of drops of vermouth to a dry martini, he set it on the bar and poured enough house red into a beaker for the waitress to pour a single glass. "I'm a bartender. People are supposed to tell me things."

"And do they? Like in the movies? I thought that was a cliché."

"It's a cliché because it happens so much. Sure,

people tell me things." He paused to mop up a puddle of melted ice. "Or sometimes they just want to have a drink and shoot the breeze. I'm easy."

"Conversationally flexible. That's a useful quality." She made him sound like someone applying for a job.

"I'm here in Orca Bay on business, that's why I'm alone."

"Got a boyfriend waiting at home?" Her ring finger was naked, but that didn't necessarily mean she was single, so he added, "Husband?"

She ran the tip of her index finger around the stem of her glass. "The truth is, I was with someone for a couple of years. I thought we might get married, but then he got a fantastic job opportunity in Geneva and I wasn't willing to leave my own job." She shrugged. "I guess he wasn't important enough."

She glanced at her BlackBerry again, wistfully. He got the strong impression that tiny package of electronics was her main connection with the outside world.

"He probably got the times mixed up if he's in Switzerland," he said, trying to cheer her up.

"Oh, no. He's with a German woman now. A pharmaceutical biochemist. She works for Bayer. In truth he wasn't much of a romantic anyway. Last year on Valentine's Day he e-mailed me a gift certificate to a kitchenware store."

"You're joking." He'd heard some sad tales of loser guys, usually from the loser guys themselves, but this was right up there.

"No. I was renovating my kitchen at the time. I thought the gift was very practical. He wouldn't know what colors or appliances I might prefer, so I was able to choose my own gift."

She had hazel eyes and the type of fair skin that burns in the sun. A sprinkling of freckles across the top of her cheeks and the bridge of her nose. Her mouth was like the rest of her. Nice without being flashy. Somehow he doubted anybody'd given her a screaming orgasm in lip-lock. Surely not kitchen-appliance boy.

"What did you give him last Valentine's Day?"

Her drink took all her concentration once more. "I booked us a weekend away at a luxury spa. Well, I had my secretary book it."

At least she'd tried to be a little more intimate in her choice of gift, though romancing people through an assistant was pretty lame.

"How long since he's been gone?"

"Frederick? He left in October."

Frederick? "Seen anybody since?"

"Romantically?" She shook her head. "My work's so crazy. It only worked with Frederick because our secretaries coordinated our schedules. Usually we managed about a week a month in the same place."

"And the romantic weekend at the spa? How did that go?"

"Very successfully, thank you."

"Frederick enjoyed his mud baths and his seaweed facial?"

"In fact, we never did coordinate our schedules. I took my mother."

That had to be about the most pathetic story he'd ever heard. Maybe he was never going to be CEO of anything, but for damn sure he was never going to need a secretary to organize his sex life. And if he ever bought a woman a kitchen appliance for Valentine's

Day he might as well crawl off somewhere to die. He'd be done.

"How about you?" she asked, startling him. Not a lot of people wanted to know about his life. Usually they were happy simply telling him about theirs. And in truth that worked for him, too. He'd rather listen than share. "Are you single?"

"Yep."

"For how long?"

He shrugged, calculating the time backward in his head. "Couple weeks."

"So recent. I'm sorry. What happened?" She regarded him with that intense, serious expression she probably got from working too much.

"Nothing dramatic. Her name was Rosalie. She was from Guatemala. Worked at the big lodge as a waitress. But she got tired of surfing and I think she was home-sick. Anyhow, she moved back home." It happened. Johnny had enjoyed Rosalie's company, but he hadn't been too sorry to see her go, either. It was part of life in a resort town. People came and went like the tide, and Johnny'd always been good at riding the waves. Another woman would come along.

The couple at the other end of the bar paid up and left, the size of the tip the guy left on the bar suggest-ing he had high hopes for the rest of the night. The way that woman was wound around him, Johnny suspected he was going to have his hopes fulfilled.

He put the credit card receipt in the till and the tip money in a jar behind him.

"Do you pool all tips or is it individual?" the woman at the bar asked.

He shot her a keen glance. "Why? You with the

IRS?" Not that he had anything to hide, but IRS people were like dentists and cops. He preferred to avoid doing business with them.

She laughed. "No. Sorry. I'm a management consultant. Sort of an efficiency expert, really, and I'm always interested in how systems work. Just idle curiosity."

"Oh. Well, don't worry. Everybody gets taken care of here. It's a good place. Fair system." A management consultant. Didn't that just fit her perfectly?

3

Sex on the Beach

1 oz vodka
1/2 oz peach schnapps
2 oz cranberry juice
2 oz orange juice

Shake together and serve over ice

SHUT UP, SHUT UP, SHUT UP! What was the matter with her, interviewing the poor bartender about their tip system. No wonder she didn't have a date on Valentine's Day, she was completely hopeless.

"Sorry," she said. "I'm a bit of a workaholic. Can't seem to turn it off."

"No problem." He gestured to her nearly empty glass. "Want another?"

She had work to do, of course, but then she always had work to do. Maybe for one night she could forget about business. After telling this stranger that her last Valentine's Day gift had been a certificate to a kitchen store, she didn't feel she could rush back to her laptop without feeling like a total loser. Besides, she was actually enjoying herself. So she didn't have a special someone, she could still go out and have fun on February fourteenth.

"Yes, but I'll try something different."

His eyes sparkled. "Okay, what'll it be?"

Not white wine, that was for sure. And every other drink she could think of sounded boring. "I have no idea. Surprise me."

He looked at her for a moment, then nodded and reached behind him for a bottle.

"Do you often match people with drinks?"

"Sure. In fact, every person is like a liquor."

Laughing, she said, "That's not true."

"Look around you." He turned back and leaned closer to her, then pointed over her shoulder toward the main dining room. "See that mellow guy with the deep voice?"

Curious, she followed the direction of Johnny's pointing finger. "The one who's a little overweight?"

"That one. He's a Baileys Irish Cream."

The notion was ridiculous, but there was something Irish-looking about the guy. The square jaw and dreamy eyes, and unfortunately he was shaped like a Baileys bottle. "Okay, I can see that."

"The elegant redhead in the corner is Chartreuse."

Wow. She could totally see that one, too. She scanned the diners looking for more of a challenge. "What about the tiny woman in the black dress two tables from the front?"

The woman seemed to stick out because she was so unlike most of the other guests immersed in romance and foreplay. She was beautiful, with dark hair and eyes, but sharp featured and plainly angry with her partner about something. Her voice was brittle and insistent, like a wasp. Surely he couldn't come up with a liquor for her.

However he did. "That's easy. She's an Italian drink. Douce Amere, it means bittersweet."

Perfect. "Well, it's an interesting way of classifying people, and I can see that it works for you."

She took the last sip of her Blue Crush while Hot Johnny regarded her in some amusement. Finally, he said, "Go ahead. Ask."

She was as transparent as the empty martini glass. She felt her lips twitch—he'd seen through her so easily. "Okay. What kind of drink am I?" And please don't say white wine, she pleaded silently. At least, not the house white.

"You're easy," he said. "You're cool and secretive on the outside, it's apparent you spend a lot of time indoors, since you're pale, but inside you're pent up effervescence dying to get out. You're classy. Expensively dressed, but not flashy. You're vintage champagne."

Even as she knew how foolish it was to fall under this charmer's spell, she couldn't help herself. She felt absurdly flattered.

"Vintage champagne, huh? Sort of a white wine."

"But so much more."

She'd been working night and day, it seemed, ever since she learned to spell her name and add two and two. Accelerated schooling, gifted programs, fast track degree program, Harvard M.B.A. by the time she was twenty-five. Now she was one of the youngest consultants in a top firm. She traveled, she diagnosed and fixed ailing companies. Business people twice her age paid a great deal of money for her opinions and nearly always tried to hire her. And here she was, having possibly the most fun Valentine's Day ever. Chatting to a bartender who didn't even know her name.

Which seemed like a terrible omission, suddenly. "It's Natalie, by the way. My name."

"Pleased to meet you, Natalie," he said, putting out his hand formally for her to shake. When their gazes connected along with their palms, she suddenly thought maybe he was enjoying his evening more than he'd expected to, as well.

Of course, he was a womanizer who slung booze for a living, but still, a man who could do *that* to a woman simply by kissing her… How could she help but steal glances at his mouth and wonder? It definitely looked like a mouth that could give a woman a very good time, not that she was any expert. He had nice lips, firm but relaxed. She knew a lot about body language, it was important in her work, and she could tell he was a relaxed person. No tension in the jaw, or the mouth, where people often held stress. Still what would this guy have to be stressed about?

She watched him toss vodka into a glass, and a few other things, then put a drink in front of her that was as fiery red in color as the Blue Crush had been cool.

"What's this one?"

"Something you need. Taste it and let me know if you like it."

She eyed the drink with suspicion. "It's not one of those dirty ones, is it? I was in a restaurant in Seattle. No, wait a minute. I think it was Denver. No, no, Pittsburgh. Anyhow, I heard this guy order a Quick…you know, a word that starts with the letter *F*."

"I promise you that is not what this is. And a quick *word that stars with the letter* F is certainly not what you need. Or anybody for that matter. Guys who order drinks like that?" He dropped his voice. "In my opinion, they have small things that start with the letter *P*."

She snorted with laughter. "I cannot believe I am having this conversation." Then she picked up her drink and sipped. The flavors were rich and bright on her tongue. Sweet and tart at the same time. Probably addictive. "Oh, yum. I like it."

"Ever had it before?"

"I don't think so. What's it called?"

His eyes challenged and warmed her. "Sex on the Beach."

"Nope, never had that."

She hadn't had the drink, either.

WHEN SHE WAS ON THE ROAD, Natalie tried to stick to her regular schedule as much as possible. She found it helped her feel that her life was somewhat in her control. Even if she wasn't in her own home, with her kitchen, her local gym or her own time zone, she could at least organize her day in some familiar way.

So, she rose at six, swam in the pool and used the hotel gym, if the hotel she was staying in had those amenities and they passed her cleanliness standards. If they didn't or, as in this case, the pool was too small for laps, she ran. This morning, however, after a night of debauchery during which she'd consumed two cocktails and chatted with the bartender as though they were old friends, she looked out of her window and saw paradise.

The bright California sunshine sparkled on waves that crashed to the shore like temper tantrums, demanding attention. The surfers were out, trying to ride that restless energy all the way in to the sand that stretched endlessly on either side.

Walking the beach wasn't nearly as cardiovascularly efficient, or as time efficient as running on the road would be, but all that energy and drama called to her.

She tied her hair back, applied extra sunscreen to skin that came to her from Swedish and Irish ancestors who'd never dreamed their genes would end up in California, put on her dark glasses and added a hat she'd bought in Sydney with sun protection right in the fabric.

The minute she hit the beach she felt happy, pausing for a moment to enjoy the view and breathe deep of the scent of ocean, something she didn't get a lot of in Chicago.

She chose a problem to mull over while she walked. Some people took iPods with them when they worked out. Natalie took a problem to solve. She was an efficiency expert, after all, so, naturally, she multitasked at every opportunity. The problem that most puzzled her was how to streamline the complicated payroll system used by the lodge she was consulting for. Problem chosen, she turned and began to stride, her sneakers sinking into the white sand.

Mentally, she was deeply tangled in the complexities of compensating contract workers, the regular payroll, the pensionables and the pensionees, when she heard a man's voice say, "Hey, where's the fire?"

"Fire? What?" She jerked to a halt, and blinked, bringing the beach into focus with difficulty. It took her a second to recognize the guy in front of her, doing what he seemed to have been doing ever since they first met last night. He was laughing at her with his eyes.

"Natalie, right?"

"Yes. And you're H… You're Johnny." What grown man still went by Johnny? And yet his boyish name suited him. He wasn't a John or a Jack. He was a laid-back, never-gonna-grow-up surfer dude. A Johnny who'd never mature into John. Cute, though.

His hair was a sun-streaked tangle, he hadn't shaved, he wore a T-shirt that she thought had once been navy and had washed out to a soft denim. His board shorts hung low on lean hips. He was carrying a battered surfboard that had plainly seen a lot of action. As, no doubt, had he. He was scruffy, unkempt and he sported an earring, something Natalie loathed on men. Yet he was the sexiest man she'd ever seen. Clearly her hormones must be out of balance.

"You're up early," he said to her, seeming in no hurry to throw himself into the pounding surf.

"I am. But I like to get a good head start on the day."

"By racewalking the beach. I noticed."

"I wasn't racewalking…." But she found she huffed the words. Then it occurred to her that while she'd been in bed well before midnight, Johnny would have had to close the bar and probably spend some downtime with his friends before getting to bed himself. "It must be even earlier for you. Did you get any sleep?"

He shrugged. "I don't need much sleep. Wastes the day."

"I agree."

He laughed. "The pace you were going, you could cover this beach in an hour. Most people take all day."

"Well, I have a lot to do and only so many days available to me."

"How long are you in town?"

"A week."

He looked down at her as though debating something, then suddenly said, "How would you like to go sailing?"

The fact that this sexy man was asking her out was such a shock she forgot for the moment that they had less than nothing in common.

"Sailing? When?"

"Today. Later. After you finish your work."

Truth was she never really finished work. On location she tended to put in sixteen-hour days, then she often dreamed of her projects and even used her exercise time to puzzle over work issues.

But the sun dancing on those waves drew her almost as magnetically as the sex appeal coming off the bartender in front of her.

"Don't you have to work tonight?"

"My night off."

"Oh. Um." She glanced at the ocean, back at him. Drew a quick breath. Knew she'd regret it but couldn't seem to stop herself saying "Okay."

"Great. Four o'clock. I'll meet you down at the main dock."

"Four o'clock. I'll be there."

He nodded and started to walk away.

"Wait."

He turned back.

"Do you have life jackets on board?"

His grin was quick and lethal. "Yep. Also, my CPR is up-to-date and I'm a trained sailor, certified all the way to open ocean. Don't worry, I won't drown you."

Feeling slightly foolish, and hoping he was telling the truth, she said, "Okay, then. See you at four."

Then she turned back to her hotel, cutting her walk short. She had a lot to do before four o'clock. And some new ideas about payroll.

The only time she'd ever been sailing was on a huge yacht one of her clients had charted on Lake Michigan. She recalled canapés and champagne and staff to do the actual sailing. Today's outing would be a lot different she suspected.

Even as she told herself not to, she watched Hot Johnny throw himself onto his board and paddle at a leisurely pace out to where the surfers congregated. Even from the shore she could see that they all knew him. Most of them must be old enough to vote and fight wars, yet they looked like a bunch of little kids out playing in the water.

As she watched, a thought struck her. Should a person be sailing on water with waves wild enough for surfing?

4

Crazy Monkey Love Martini

1 oz rum
1/2 oz banana liqueur
1/2 oz caramel toffee liqueur
1 tsp white peach puree
Cranberry juice to taste

Serve over ice.

ON THE POSITIVE SIDE, Natalie decided when she got to the dock at 4 p.m. precisely, the sailboat wasn't as small as she'd feared. In fact, it looked to be close to thirty feet long, much larger than the dingy with a sail she'd imagined.

She had no trouble spotting Johnny since he was standing right beside his boat. Chatting to a tall, gorgeous model type who could easily be mistaken for Naomi Campbell.

"Hey," he said, waving to her as her steps faltered. "You're right on time." He took in her jean shorts and long-sleeved T-shirt with barely a glance. "Natalie, this is Rita. She's my competition in the Orca Bay Martini Contest."

The woman made a tsking sound. "I kicked his ass last year. I intend to do the same again."

"Martini competition?" She vaguely remembered seeing something about it in the visitor's guide in her room, but it was hard to concentrate. Rita wore white micro shorts, a red tank top that showed off every line of her statuesque body. Her full mouth shimmered with a mocha lipstick and her makeup was bold and flaw-lessly applied. Beside her, Natalie had never felt so pale and colorless. She wondered if this was going to be a sailing trio and whether it would be too blatant to feign sudden illness.

"It's a competition to create the new martini of the year. All the local bars, restaurants and hotels get involved. For fifteen years your man there won the martini competition." Her smile flashed white and sharklike. "Then I came along."

"Once," Johnny said, looking serious for the first time since Natalie had first seen him. "You got lucky once. I'll be ready for you this year."

"I already have my drink figured out," Rita told him. "It's gonna knock your socks off—" she looked down at his feet "—if you ever wore any."

"I admit I was complacent. Made it easy for you to steal my trophy, but not this year, babe. I'm taking back what's mine."

"When is the competition?" Natalie asked.

"Next Friday night."

She was booked until the end of next week, scheduled to leave Saturday. She'd be here. "Can anyone go?"

"Yep," Johnny said. "All the bars are selling tickets. Proceeds go to Orca whale conservation. It's a good cause. You should come."

"Definitely."

Rita glanced at her watch. "In the meantime, you come up and see me in the bar at the Hennington Lodge. I'll make you a martini."

"Thanks, I will. I'm staying at the lodge, actually."

"You two have fun. Think I'll go polish my trophy." With a wave of her long, elegant hand, Rita strutted off up the dock.

Johnny watched his long-legged competitor but Natalie didn't think it was with unbridled lust. Not that she was any expert. "She's from L.A.," he said, as though that explained anything. "Her drinks are flashy. All glamour, not enough substance."

He turned back to Natalie. "So, ready to put your life in my hands?"

Terrifying choice of words, no doubt deliberate. But it was a gorgeous afternoon, the waves had died down considerably since the morning and she was a strong swimmer. Besides, he did say the boat had life jackets. "Yes," she said. "I'm ready."

And, after she got used to sailing, it was fun and more active than she'd imagined. "You ever sailed before?" he shouted back at her from where he was tightening a rope.

"No."

"You gonna keep watching my every move like a hawk or do you want to do something useful?"

"Useful," she yelled back, feeling stray strands of hair flap against her face in the breeze.

So she learned the rudiments of tacking, and how to move fast to avoid the boom, a bit about steering and in all the afternoon, she never once thought about bringing the venerable Hennington Lodge up to the most modern standards of efficiency, not their payroll, their marketing, front desk, or their old-fashioned management style.

Johnny never made her feel stupid or clumsy; he explained things to her, laughed when she made mistakes and was lavish with his praise when she got it right, which made her relax.

When the sun was getting close to setting, he said, "Do you want to have dinner?"

She was starving, she realized. He'd showed her down below where there was a tiny galley, an even tinier head and room to sleep six very friendly people.

"What, here?"

"No. My place."

"Where do you live?"

He pointed behind him. "There."

She squinted and saw a modest beach house sitting in a private cove with its own dock.

"In that beach house? You live there?"

"Yep."

He either had a lot of roommates, she figured, or he was getting a killer deal on the rent. Not bad digs for a surfer boy bartender.

"Wow. Sure."

They tied up the boat and she followed him down the wooden dock to the beach. The house was modest, gray and covered with weathered wood siding so you could easily miss it if you scanned the coastline from the sea. It was tucked back as though it were shy to be so understated in such a spectacular setting.

He walked right up from the beach onto a big wooden deck with a barbecue, beat-up wooden table and deck chairs and opened French doors that hadn't been locked. She entered, her curiosity growing. Inside, the house was small but functional, and everything faced the double French doors that led to the deck. And the view.

The main room was open concept, with a small but efficient kitchen that looked as though it was put together from Home Depot or IKEA components, a sitting area that was also clean and simple containing a battered oak table and chairs, dark blue comfy couches, the smallest TV she'd ever seen in a man's living space.

The decor was pretty much beachcomber. Old glass floats, a coffee table built of driftwood, a couple of bottles crusted with age and years at the bottom of the ocean. A few shells along a windowsill.

"It's beautiful," she said, her eye drawn, as every visitor's must be, to the view.

"Thanks."

"Do you have roommates?"

"Not anymore."

"Oh." She looked around. "Um, bathroom?"

He pointed to the left and she excused herself. The bathroom was clean and as modern as the one in her apartment.

She was dying to ask him who owned this place, but decided it was really none of her business. So, she stifled her nosiness and used her energy instead on trying to tame the mess that the wind had made of her hair. Even through the sunscreen she'd caught a little glow, but it wasn't bad, and even, she thought, made her look healthier than normal.

Emerging she found her host rustling inside the fridge. "I have fresh halibut, and some other stuff if you hate fish."

"No. I love it. What can I do?"

"Salad?"

"Sure."

While she washed and chopped greens, he went outside and fired up the barbecue. Coming back he pulled out a bottle of white wine from the fridge. "Wine?"

"What? No rainbow colored cocktails?" she teased.

"Can if you want. But it's my day off."

She laughed. "Wine's great. Thanks."

She carried the salad outside and wondered if a woman had chosen the simple, bright-colored china, and the matching place mats. Maybe Rosalie from Guatemala? Not that it was any of her business, either. She was only here for a week, so what did she care?

The food was as good as anything Natalie had ever tasted, mostly because she was so hungry, and the sea air sharpened her appetite.

"It's so quiet here," she marveled. She loved that he hadn't cranked up the music the second he got in the door, or flipped on the TV for CNN the way Frederick used to, as though every happening in the world were somehow his vital and immediate business.

Johnny looked at her strangely. "Quiet? Are you kidding? The sea lions are barking their heads off, the gulls are going nuts and the ocean pretty much never shuts up. It's always noisy here."

"But you don't hear traffic or people or even music. It's heaven." She turned her head to look at him, sitting back in a wooden Adirondack chair.

"So, tell me about Natalie," he said.

"Not much to tell," she admitted. "You already know about Frederick. And my job. I grew up in Chicago, where I still live. Have two brothers."

"Family there?"

She shook her head. "My parents retired to Florida a couple of years back. One of my brothers is a doctor in Boca Raton, so they moved there for the sunshine and to get to see the grandchildren. My other brother is an investment banker in Manhattan."

"Wow. High achievers."

"I guess. My dad was a psychiatrist and my mom was a math professor, so we pretty much grew up between analysis and pop quizzes."

He stopped chewing and stared at her. "You're kidding, right?"

"Mostly, but our parents definitely prepared us to succeed in the world."

"They must be proud."

"I think they'd be happier if I settled down." She shrugged uncomfortably. "Thirty's looming, I've got the career, now they figure it's time for the husband and kids."

"What do you think?"

"That I'm fine the way I am, thanks."

He looked slightly relieved.

"How about you? Have you always lived in California?"

"Born and bred. I grew up in San Diego. I like being near the water. Only time I've ever left is to go to Hawaii or Australia to surf."

"Wow. Imagine traveling for fun," she said, hearing the wistfulness in her own voice. When she traveled for fun it was usually tacking a couple of extra days onto a business trip. Paris for the weekend after she was exhausted from a week of meetings in London. A few days in the Bahamas after Frederick closed a deal in

New York. When was the last time she had gone on a true, honest-to-goodness holiday?

"Natalie, I don't know you very well, but I get the feeling you need to take it easy more. Try living in the moment."

She could answer, she could explain that she took yoga, but then she'd probably get all honest and have to admit that even when she meditated, her mind usually drifted to whatever project she was working on. Which was not where her mind was, apparently, supposed to go during meditation.

While they lingered over wine, the sun set, exploding with hot colors that suffused the sky with all the hues of passion.

And suddenly it was dark.

"That was a great moment," she said softly, feeling alive in every cell of her body, and realizing that her mind hadn't been drifting at all as they'd watched the sunset together. She'd been as much in the now, in her body, and in the moment as any yoga teacher could ask.

"Every moment can be a great moment," Johnny said softly. She didn't realize he'd left his own chair, but now she saw that he was standing by hers, close to her. So close he could reach out and touch her face, tilt her chin, let her know he was going to kiss her and give her time to move away.

She didn't move away. She closed her eyes and waited.

And when his mouth touched hers she felt the way the sun had when it exploded into fiery passion before bedding down for the night.

5

G-Spot

1 oz Chambord
1 oz Southern Comfort
1 oz orange juice

Combine ingredients in a cocktail shaker with ice. Shake and strain into shot glasses.

HIS KISS HAD THE SAME IMPACT as those cocktails he'd served her last night. So seductive on the tongue that she didn't notice how intoxicating they were.

He pulled her up and she went, wrapping her arms around his neck, pressing her body against his. He tilted his head, and as he did so she felt the brush of stubble against her cheek.

As he deepened the kiss, she opened her mouth to him while having the oddest sensation that she wanted to open up to him completely, something she'd never wanted to do with a man before. Not ones she'd known months or even years, never mind twenty-four hours.

The ocean lapped away behind them, sounding to her rapidly clouding senses as though it were panting.

A breeze whispered against her bare arms and she

heard sand brushing across the deck's surface. When she breathed in she smelled the ocean. And Johnny. He spent so much time on and in and around the sea that he smelled a little like it. Of salt and fresh air and the mysterious tang of the ocean.

He kissed as though it was what he'd been put on earth to do. She couldn't have said what made him so special; it wasn't that he did anything other men hadn't done. He pressed his lips on hers. Big deal. Why did it feel as if something magical was happening to her? He used his tongue, but not the way some guys did, as if they'd lost something down her throat and were searching for it. Instead, he licked and toyed with her, tempting and teasing, clearly enjoying her response as much as she did. Unbidden, she recalled the conversation she'd overheard about him. Oh, if there was a man who could make a woman orgasm by kissing her mouth, Johnny was that man.

His body was warm and hard against hers. He was moving his hands restlessly over her back, lower with each pass until he gripped her hips.

The blood was singing in her ears, her heart hammering away as arousal built fast, much faster than anything she'd ever experienced. Certainly Frederick had never had her panting with need within minutes. But then he'd been the first to admit he had a low sex drive. He'd mentioned it almost as a matter of pride, as though not wasting a lot of time on sex was one more convenience in a very time-efficient life.

He seemed to believe they were matched in that regard. After a few months she had started to lose her enthusiasm. Maybe she'd even believed she didn't have much of a sex drive, either.

Boy was she wrong.

Raw sexual need was making places on her body ache that she didn't even know could ache. Like the soles of her feet. When had they become size-seven sex organs? She must have missed that lesson in basic anatomy in high school.

Not just the soles, either. Her toes felt restless and twitchy. Her legs were beginning to tremble, her stomach was jumpy, her breasts so sensitive that the feel of their clothed bodies rubbing together was making her almost delirious; where he was stroking her back, it was starting to hum, and her actual sex organs were firing on all cylinders.

He pulled away from her only enough to get his hands under her shirt, teasing upward until he could touch her breasts. He never stopped kissing her. Sexual multitasking at its best. He reached around to undo her bra and when his fingers slid around her ribs and he touched her breasts she moaned deep in her throat.

"Want to stay out here or go inside?" he whispered to her, nibbling on her ear while his mouth was there anyway.

There wasn't even a suggestion that she wouldn't sleep with him, and much as she wanted to have sex with this man, so much in fact that her body was on fire, her mind, that much more central organ to her life to date, kicked in.

She pulled back.

Her mouth was wet from his kisses, cool where the breeze blew against her lips like a cold kiss of reality. What was she doing? This wasn't her style at all.

"Shouldn't we talk about this?" she asked, appalled

at how breathy she sounded, as if she was in the middle of a bad asthma attack with no puffer.

His hand was so warm and it never stopped stroking her breasts, so it was tough to concentrate. "Talk about what?" He didn't sound as though he was in respiratory distress, more as though he'd just woken up from a deep sleep. Slow and pleased with himself.

In the moments before she spoke again, she contemplated letting nature take its course, as part of her wanted so badly to do. Just blindly go at it and who cares about tomorrow? But she'd never been that kind of woman, doubted she ever would be.

The water continued to lap behind her, and the breeze played with her skin and hair, as light and teasing as Johnny's fingers playing so skillfully at her breasts.

"I—um, what exactly are we doing here?"

It was so dark she could only vaguely make out his features, so close to her own, but even in the dim light she thought she saw a flash of humor glint in his eyes.

"We're doing what comes naturally."

"Maybe to you," she muttered, then felt like an idiot for blurting out something so stupid.

"Sex isn't natural for you?" Now he sounded genuinely confused, as if she'd confessed she had trouble eating or some sleep disorder.

"Johnny, this is only our first date."

His hands stilled, then slid down off her breasts, tracking down her belly to rest lightly on her hips, and she fought the urge to grab them and plant them back where she wanted them. "I'm not, uh, much for dating."

Did she have the terminology wrong? If a man asked a woman to go sailing and took her back to his place for dinner, was that not a date? "What are you into?"

He shrugged. She could feel the movement even though he was barely touching her anymore. "I don't know. Hanging out. Hooking up. Nothing too serious."

Hanging out? Wasn't that what kids did at the mall? He wasn't that young. Maybe there was a language barrier between Chicago and California. Or, more likely, she thought, between Johnny and her, but she was able to translate his meaning. "You don't think sex is serious?"

He backed up a step, letting his hands fall from her hips so now they were two completely separate people standing several feet apart. "Hey, I was planning on using protection. I'm not talking about making babies or anything."

She almost laughed, except from the slight tone of desperation she got the feeling that maybe he'd been approached the odd time as a human sperm bank. Come to think of it, the number of babies in this town toted around by young people who didn't look old enough to drink, never mind raise children, did seem disproportionately large.

"I'm not talking about babies, either. I would expect you to be scrupulous about protection." Oh, great, now she was using big words, a sure sign that she was riled. "I certainly am. Fastidious, I mean." The twin specters of unwanted pregnancy and STDs meant that she insisted on condoms even though she was on birth control pills. At least until her partner and she were both thoroughly tested and clearly monogamous. Something Johnny blatantly wasn't.

"Okay, then." But he stayed where he was and still seemed confused.

She was starting to feel confused, too, and a little irritated. "Sex is the most intimate act two people can share. Shouldn't we get to know each other first?"

"How much do we need to know? You're a good-looking woman. You're smart, funny. Seem like you've got your head screwed on right. Isn't that enough?"

"No. What do I know about you? You mix delicious drinks, as far as I can judge, you're a competent sailor, you can cook." She felt herself begin to blush in the dark. "And you're a great kisser."

His teeth gleamed as he grinned at her. "Not that I want to blow my own horn here, but I should mention that I'm pretty good in the sack. In case, you know, you think that's relevant."

Somehow, she'd pretty much guessed that. And that if she walked away she was probably turning down a night she would remember her whole life.

Truth was, she seemed fated to end up with a man like Frederick, which whom she had everything in common from education to ambition. Similar jobs, similar career paths. They'd end up in a big city where they both continued to climb the corporate ladder; they'd entertain other power couples in training. They'd probably program sex into their BlackBerries in case they got so busy they forgot.

No, a man like that wasn't going to bring a woman to climax by kissing her. Certainly not this woman.

For a second she considered trying tonight Johnny's way. Hang out, hook up and be done with it. But she didn't do casual sex. And even if she decided to break that cardinal rule for one too-sexy bartender, she couldn't break it now, after she'd had a heady day of sailing, wine and fantastic kisses.

Before she could indulge in spontaneous sex she was going to have to think about it. Long and hard.

"I feel a little foolish. But I didn't know we were going to spend the evening together. I didn't plan, I'm not sure—"

"Hey, don't get bent out of shape. It's no big deal."

And she could tell by his breezy tone that to him it wasn't a big deal. Have sex with the business traveler in town for a week, or don't. If not her, tomorrow there'd be another woman eager to share his bed. Hell, it wasn't even that late. He could go downtown as soon as he was rid of her, hang out and get hooked up again within the hour.

"Okay then." She licked her lips, wondering how to smooth over the moment and realizing there wasn't a way.

They were done. Dinner was over. He'd moved on to foreplay and instead of ending up making love, she'd turned the event into foreplay interruptis. There was nowhere to go from here but home.

Well, back to her hotel which was as close as she could get to home in Orca Bay.

She looked around as though to spot her purse, but all she saw were the dark shapes of the minimal deck furniture. She didn't have a purse with her anyway, nothing but a straw bag she'd bought in the hotel gift shop because she didn't think her briefcase was the appropriate carrier for her sweatshirt and her wallet and hairbrush. All she'd brought with her. "I should probably get going." She headed past him and into the house. He came behind her and switched on a lamp, so the room leaped into view, lit so suddenly the brightness made her squint. There was her bag lying casually, oh, so much more casually than its new owner, on the blue couch.

"Do you have the number of a cab company?" she asked as she retrieved her bag.

"Yeah, sure." He walked into the light and she felt momentarily awkward. They'd been wound around each other only minutes ago, panting and groping and now he was a near stranger again. "There's only one cab company so they get busy sometimes, but hopefully it's a quiet night." Since she was standing with her hand on the black rotary dial phone on his battered oak desk, he didn't offer to call her a cab, simply recited the number from memory. As she leaned over she realized her bra was riding high, still unfastened. She must look ridiculous. She made the call, keeping her shoulders rolled.

"Orca Bay Cab Company," a cheerful voice told her.

"Yes, I'd like a cab please."

"I'm all booked up for at least another hour. Can you wait?"

Oh, for goodness sake. Could this one thing not be easy? "Um, I'll call you back."

"Sure thing."

She hung up the phone.

Johnny was in his kitchen pouring a glass of water. "Problem?"

"They're booked up for an hour."

"I'd drive you back if I had a car."

"You don't have a car?" The words were blurted before she could stop them. Who didn't even own a car? He couldn't be that poor, could he? Was the boat even his? Maybe people didn't tip bartenders the way they did waitstaff. All this went through her head even as she thought what a long hour it was going to be before the cab got there.

"I hate cars. Too much greenhouse gas."

Oh, so it was an environmental decision. Or at least that was his story. Not that she didn't believe in saving the environment, but she'd happily buy a few carbon credits if it would get her home any earlier.

"Want some water?"

"Sure." While his back was turned, she refastened her bra. "I guess I'd better phone the cab company back."

"Why don't you borrow my bike?"

"Your bike?"

"It's how I get around."

"Ride a bike back to town?"

"It's a fifteen-minute ride tops. I've got a light and everything for night riding. It's perfectly safe."

"Are the tires pumped up?"

"Of course. I ride it all the time."

"Helmet?"

His eyes were laughing at her again. She didn't care. Protecting her brain from injury was more important than being laughed at. "Yeah. Helmet." He looked her up and down. "You do know how to ride a bike?"

"Well, I haven't for a few years," she had to admit. "But—"

"Riding a bike is like sex. You never forget."

She gulped. "Okay."

Why not? It would get her out of here sooner. She didn't think she could manage an hour's small talk, not if he was going to say teasing things about sex. And if they ran out of things to talk about, she had a bad, bad feeling she'd end the evening "hooking up."

6

Pacific Blue

1 oz mango rum
1 oz pineapple rum
1 oz blue curaçao
Fill with 7-Up

Directions: In a tall glass filled with ice, add blue
curaçao and rum. Fill rest of glass with 7-Up and
stir. Garnish glass with an orchid and paper
umbrella.

CRUISING DOWN the Pacific Highway was exhilarat-
ing she discovered once she got on her way. They'd
muddled through getting her organized for her big
trek. Sliding on the red helmet, making sure the bike
wasn't too big for her. It wasn't. A sleek, black road
bike, it was much nicer and clearly more expensive
than the rusty, yard-sale three-speed she'd dreaded.
He kept the bike in an old wooden garage out back
by the road.

She'd worried about an awkward goodbye, but in
truth she was the only one who'd found their farewell
uncomfortable.

"Well," she said, once she was all ready to go, "Thanks for a wonderful day."

"I had fun," he said, then kissed her briefly on the lips. A kiss that was a little more than friendly, but not much more. "Drive safe."

Because he watched as she wheeled her way up the steep driveway, there was no way she was going to let him see her wobble from side to side up the hill. There were certain things she performed extremely well under pressure. Business presentations in particular. However, riding an unfamiliar bicycle up a steep driveway while under the eye of the sexiest man she'd ever turned down was not one of them.

Once on the main road, she'd climbed on and within a couple of minutes the bike was as natural feeling as when she'd ridden constantly as a kid.

Why had she given up something she loved so much she wondered as she followed the road that hugged the Pacific.

She owned a bike. Not as nice as this one, but an attractive midpriced green hybrid. She hadn't ridden in probably four years. Too busy. Or out of town.

Always so busy.

Although there was little traffic, still she hugged the shoulder, making sure she was visible at all times. A couple of people waved as they drove by. One honked the horn—three short blasts in a row. For a second she thought she'd committed some unforgivable traffic violation. Until she realized that in the dark, wearing his helmet and riding his bike, she'd been mistaken for Johnny the bartender who was a popular character around town.

She loved riding alongside the ocean. Sure, Chicago

was lakeside, but it wasn't the same. It was the smell, she thought, and the ever-changing tides that made the ocean so special.

Riding the bike gave her a feeling similar to the one she'd had earlier when they'd been sailing. As if the movement was natural and at times effortless. Although, as she peddled her way around a bend in the road she realized this was a first. She'd been transported home late at night by owner-driven car, by chauffer-driven limousine, by cab and on one memorable occasion by helicopter, but never, ever had she borrowed some guy's bike. Well, at least he hadn't offered her his skateboard.

He was right, though; she pedaled up to Hennington Lodge a mere quarter of an hour after she'd left Johnny's place, feeling invigorated. She didn't remember a day when she'd had quite so much fresh air and exercise.

Of course, she had no idea what to do with the bike. She couldn't take it inside the hotel lobby, and she was terrified to leave the bike outside in case it got stolen. Finally, she propped it against the wall beside the door and running in, grabbed the bellboy standing in the lobby. He promised to put it in a storage locker for her, gave her a numbered ticket and she waited until she'd seen him wheel it away.

Only then did she realize she was still wearing Johnny's bike helmet. As she removed it, she realized something else. He wasn't going to be able to go pick up some other woman tonight. She had his only means of transportation.

And how was he going to get to work tomorrow?

She'd have to phone him.

She rushed into her room, dropped the helmet on the bed and dug through the hotel desk drawer for the phone directory. She'd already pulled it out and set it on the desktop when she realized she had no idea what Johnny's last name was. She'd contemplated having sex with a guy named Hot Johnny, no last name. When she got home she was making an appointment for a complete physical checkup.

And she'd better have a mental one, too, while she was at it.

Her fingers tapped restlessly against the desktop. She solved complicated problems all the time. Finding Johnny's number was not complicated. Just tricky.

She looked all over his bike helmet, but wasn't really surprised to find he hadn't labeled his equipment with his name and phone number.

The place to begin was with the Driftwood where he worked. She was fairly certain that no one would give out an employee's home number and she didn't want to embarrass Johnny by explaining the situation. Not that he seemed to be the discreet type, but she thought it best to err on the side of caution. Who could she possibly get his phone number from?

She pondered for a few minutes and suddenly remembered Rita, the gorgeous rival bartender. She'd already seen them together. The woman worked right here at the Hennington Lodge, she'd said.

Natalie picked up the phone and soon found herself speaking to Rita for the second time that day. "I'm not sure if you remember me, but I was with Johnny earlier. We met at the dock."

"Of course I remember you. You're not his usual type."

Having no idea what to make of that, Natalie thought it best to ignore the comment. "I wonder if I could ask you a favor. I need Johnny's phone number and I can't find it in the book."

"Johnny Santini? Aren't you with him?"

"No. I'm in my room, and I need to return something to him. I forgot to get his number."

There was a slight pause. "You're not at his place and he's not in yours?"

"No."

A low, delighted chuckle greeted her. "Like I said, you're not his usual type."

"Of course he didn't strike out. I mean…" She sighed irritably. Why the hell hadn't she memorized the number on his ridiculous ancient rotary dial phone? "I have to be up early, so I came back to the hotel."

"Hey, not my business." But she still sounded as though she were enjoying a private joke. "I've got his number here somewhere."

In the background, Natalie could hear the sounds of activity, voices talking and dishes rattling. She wondered if the phone was in the kitchen.

"Here you go," and she read out the phone number.

"Thanks, Rita."

"Tell him I said 'hi.'" And she was gone.

Oh, dear.

Well, she had the number now, she might as well use it. She called and after five rings, when she pictured the old black phone shrilling away in his house, Johnny finally picked up. "Yeah," he said.

"Hi. It's Natalie."

"Change your mind?" She almost smiled at the light, teasing tone in his voice.

"No. I wanted to make arrangements to get your bike back to you. What time do you need it tomorrow?"

"No biggie. I'll grab a ride into work. Why don't you bring it down sometime when I'm there? I start work at four."

"Sure. Okay. Um, where do I park it?"

"I'll show you when you get there."

"Okay. See you tomorrow."

"Sure."

"Um. I really had a good time today."

He chuckled, as though she had made a joke. "Me, too."

"Okay, then. I'll see you tomorrow."

She hung up the phone and looked around for something to do. It was only ten after ten at night. Not really late enough for bed, but too late to work. Besides, she had a lot of free-floating energy in her bloodstream that she knew was sexual. She needed to do something. She could work out, but she'd had plenty of exercise today.

Then the oddest idea popped into her mind. Hennington Lodge had a nice lounge off the restaurant. It was right downstairs and Rita was working. She could go down to Rita and beg her not to tease Johnny about his date running off on him so early. Not that she considered a six-hour date short, but the locals in Orca Bay clearly lived by a different set of rules than she did.

The second she thought of sitting alone at yet another bar, chatting to yet another bartender, this one a female, she was opening the hotel closet and reaching for a pair of white jeans. She threw a navy sweater over top of her T-shirt, snugged into the jeans and stepped into walking sandals.

Brush her teeth and hair, swipe on some colored lip gloss, grab the straw bag and she was out of there.

As she'd half hoped, half feared, Rita was working alone behind the bar. The Hennington was classy, a spa and lodge that catered to well-to-do tourists and boaters, few of whom were relaxing out in the bar the night after Valentine's Day. Glancing around, she somehow knew this wasn't a place where locals hung out. Maybe that was something else she could discuss with management. She felt certain that most guests wouldn't guess that the lodge wasn't doing as well as it should, or running as effectively; the place was gorgeous, luxurious, quiet in the most expensive way. And with her help it would soon become as efficient as possible.

Rita raised an eyebrow when Natalie hiked herself up onto one of the carved wooden bar stools. "Hey, girlfriend. What can I get you?"

"Oh. I don't know." She glanced at the thousand or so bottles on the wall and didn't feel like any of them. "Do you have herbal tea?"

"Of course." Rita didn't give her a hard time, or send her to the coffee shop. "If you're looking for something to make you sleepy, I've got a nice chamomile," she said, as though she knew that the woman who walked away from Hot Johnny was going to need a lot of help sleeping.

"Great."

The tea came up a minute later in a narrow glass Bodum on a tray, with a silver spoon and a plate holding a tiny dish of honey and a lemon wedge. She let it steep for a minute then pushed down the plunger and poured the fragrant tea into a white china cup.

"How was sailing?" Rita asked.

"It was beautiful."

"He's got a nice boat." She said it in a neutral way that could almost be taken as a double meaning. Substitute anything you like for the word *boat*.

"Yes. Yes, he does." She sipped the tea.

Rita cut up a lime and replenished a tray of them sitting in front of her.

"Is there a bartender-customer privilege?" she asked.

"Come again?"

"You know, like doctors and lawyers have with their patients and clients? If we talk about something, will you keep it confidential?"

"Oh, you mean like the confessional?"

"Exactly."

Rita shook her head, her black hair swinging. "No, there's nothing like that. At least, not officially. But if you're asking me to keep my mouth shut, I will." She rested her elbows on the bar. "You look like you need to talk and right now I'm so bored I'm going out of my mind."

"It's about Johnny."

"Thought it might be."

She glanced up and back down at her tea. "I didn't sleep with him."

"You being here drinking tea suggested that to me."

"You won't tell anybody, will you? That he struck out, I mean?"

Rita's all-knowing smile could have hung in the Louvre. "Honey, most women wouldn't say it was Johnny who struck out."

"I know. I wanted to." She released a breath that came out as a heartfelt sigh. "I really wanted to. But I didn't. And now I'm wondering why."

"Well, I've never tried him out myself, but he's got a rep, that's for sure. Johnny's a good-time guy. He likes women. Easy on the eyes. If you're not looking for serious, you could do worse."

"I'm only here for another week and a half. You don't think getting involved with someone for such a short time is…slutty?"

Rita's laugh was as sexy as the rest of her. "This is Orca Bay. Nobody's going to tell on you to your mom."

"I know, but…oh, I think it's this town. It's too relaxing or something. Normally I'm so engrossed in work I barely notice my surroundings."

"It might not be the town that's too relaxing. It might be Johnny who's too hot."

"Well, then there's that."

"Look, I can't tell you what to do. You're a big girl. But if you came here tonight looking for information I can tell you he's not a man who hurts a woman on purpose. He stays with one woman at a time, maybe not a long time, but while they're together, they're together, you know? He's decent."

She nodded. Decent was good.

"Johnny and me, we've got this competition going between us, but I know if I need anything I could go to him and he'd help me, no questions asked. I can't say that about a lot of people." She paused. "Well, maybe there are a lot of people who'd help me out, but most of them I wouldn't ask. The thing with Johnny is you can trust him."

"That's quite a recommendation."

"I don't give it lightly. Remember what I said, though, if you're looking for forever, look somewhere else."

The thought of her and Johnny forever was enough to bring a genuine smile to her face. "No. I can see we wouldn't be much of a fit, long-term."

"If you're looking for some no-strings-attached fun for a few days, Johnny is your man. And you look to me like you are in dire need of a little fun."

"It would be against everything I've ever believed about myself. It would be like indulging a whim, a scene out of someone else's life, a…"

"Fantasy?"

Her gaze snapped to Rita's. "Oh, my. You're right. He's like my ultimate sexual fantasy. Sex with a stranger." Then she slapped a hand over her mouth, feeling her eyes go round. "I can't believe I said that out loud."

"Relax. You wouldn't be human if you didn't dream of something…a little different from the ordinary."

"But having a completely frivolous affair with a man I only want for sex would be…" She started to giggle. "It would be amazing."

"How many women ever get to enjoy their fantasy come to life?"

Maybe Rita was right.

The idea, which had seemed so incredible, grew on her.

Why shouldn't she indulge in a beach fling? People did it all the time and nothing terrible happened to them.

She glanced down. The steam from the remaining tea in the glass carafe made shifting patterns on the glass. "Maybe he won't give me another chance."

"And maybe he will. You'll never know until you try."

Natalie gnawed on her lip, an annoying habit she thought she'd cured herself of. "I'm not usually indecisive."

"You don't have to decide anything tonight. There isn't going to be a test with right answers and wrong answers. Sleep on it."

"You're right. Thanks. You know, I spend a lot of my time giving advice. It's nice to get some for a change."

"What brings you to Orca Bay?"

"My work. I'm a management consultant. Hired by your hotel to improve efficiency."

"I hear that term, but I never know what it means."

"We try to fix specific problems, streamline systems, sometimes we help organizations through change or get brought in for short-term projects. There's an entire section of my company that does nothing but update and train in new technologies."

"Wow. I get bored just hearing about it."

"Well, it can be very exciting. We like to think of ourselves as doctors, making sick companies well. I consult, diagnose the problem and give advice on fixing it."

"In my line of work, I give a lot of advice, too. Mostly, I listen."

"Listening is a key skill," Natalie said, nodding in agreement. "Sometimes companies think they have a certain type of problem, but actually it's something else that's messing things up."

Rita's lips tilted ever so slightly. "People are like that, too."

"Yes. I guess you're right. Well, that chamomile is working. I'm getting sleepy." She hauled herself off the bar stool. "Thanks for this. I appreciate it."

"Anytime. I'm usually here. And good luck."

"Thanks."

As Rita had suggested, she decided to sleep on her problem. Which was, did she want to explore a short-term, no-strings-attached affair with a very attractive guy.

First she thought, yes, why not?

Then she thought, no. Flings weren't for her.

Then she thought, how would she know? She'd never had a fling.

She hadn't had sex in a while, either. Not since Frederick, and truth to tell, she was feeling as though she really needed some sex. Adequate, Frederick-style sex would do, but Hot Johnny, have-an-orgasm-while-kissing sex was alarmingly tempting. When she remembered the way she'd felt in his arms earlier tonight, she realized that this needing-sex urge hadn't existed eight hours ago.

Seemed that it was specifically Johnny who was making her crazy with wanting.

Well, maybe she was like one of the companies she helped. She had a certain problem in one area, and why not go to an expert consultant for help?

She was grinning to herself as she fell asleep thinking of Johnny as a sex consultant.

She only hoped he was still interested in the job.

7

Johnny-come-lately

1 oz. Grand Marnier
1 oz. crème de noyaux
1 1/2 oz. whiskey
1 oz. cranberry juice

Build over rocks in a highball glass.

JOHNNY WOKE UP to his favorite sound in the world. Waves. Some men loved the mountains, some the rolling farm country, some the desert, and he respected their choices. But for him, it would always be the ocean.

He'd left the French doors in his bedroom wide-open as he usually did when he slept. Apart from the odd visit by wandering cats and once a disoriented seagull, the system worked. He preferred fresh air to air-conditioning, only shutting the doors when rain was pelting, night grew too cold, or he had a woman who didn't love the idea that she was all but sleeping on the beach.

As he rolled over to his back and yawned, he wondered how Natalie would have felt about the door open versus door closed discussion. With a shake of his head he realized it was unlikely he'd ever find out.

Cracking his jaw on a second enormous yawn, he shambled out to the kitchen.

He was in the middle of eating his breakfast, whole wheat cereal and fresh oranges, outside on the deck with his newspaper spread in front of him, when a familiar figure came out of his house.

"Help yourself to some coffee," Johnny said.

"Thanks," Ben Cheung said, easing his lanky body into the opposite chair.

Ben and he had known each other since they first started out working in the same restaurant back in San Diego. Johnny had become a bartender while Ben had worked construction days, and waited table nights until the construction part swallowed the rest. Now, fifteen years later, he had his own construction company, Cheung Builders, as displayed on the navy baseball cap he was wearing. Ben had brought his company with him when he relocated to Orca Bay a couple of years back.

Ben Cheung was the product of a Hong Kong banker father and a Texas beauty queen. He had neither the business savvy of the one, nor the extravagant good looks of the other, but a combination of the two that worked pretty well for him. If his father was disappointed that his son hadn't pursued the Ivy League education he'd planned on, he'd been amply rewarded by the daughter who had graduated summa cum laude from Stanford and was now a top executive in the computer industry. Ben had always been more interested in surfing than studying, but he was nobody's fool.

He and Johnny were alike in that way. They never talked about it, but they were closer than brothers.

"Did you tell Helen I'd be coming by this morning?" Ben asked.

Buying the apartment building had been more of a spur of the moment decision than his first venture into real estate—buying his house. He'd come across the beach cottage, fortunately for him, during one of the periodic dips in the real estate market, fallen in love with it, and because he wasn't into a lot of material junk, he'd had a good chunk of change already saved up. Enough for a down payment.

Having a mortgage bugged him. So he'd worked extra hours, bartended at private gigs and for rich dudes on fancy boats. He'd paid off the mortgage in five years.

He hadn't planned on buying more property, but his friend Helen lived in a nearby apartment building with her kids. It was a cool old building with an original art deco lobby. When it had gone up for sale, she'd been terrified she'd lose her home because everybody who looked at it wanted to tear the place down and replace it with a luxury condo—whose units would have been priced far out of the reach of Helen and most of the other tenants.

Johnny wasn't the sort who went to public meetings and protested development. Instead, he had a talk with his bank manager and then went to see the fellow who owned the building, who also didn't want to see it turned into condos.

So Johnny bought the building, helped Ben fix up the suites and Helen became the building caretaker, and most of the residents stayed on because he didn't gouge them on rent. The rents covered all his expenses and made him a small profit. Meanwhile the value of the property had skyrocketed.

"Yeah, yeah," Johnny said. "She warned the tenants you'd be poking around today."

"Good. I think you're smart to do the windows at the same time as the balconies. Get all the hassle out of the way quickly so the tenants don't complain so much."

"We gave them lots of warning, I think they're cool," Johnny said, stretching his arms above his head.

"You don't charge enough for rent," Ben commented.

Johnny shrugged. "Don't have much turnover. To me that's worth it."

"You're lazy, man!"

"I know."

"Loads of caretakers would take that job for free rent, and you pay Helen, as well. It's crazy," Ben said.

"She does a great job."

"You'll end up putting her kids through college. You realize that."

"They're good kids," Johnny replied. "And it's not your money, so why do you care?"

"I just hate wasting money."

"I should charge you for the amount of coffee you drink."

"There's a difference between being smart with your money and being cheap. Besides, this is the best coffee in town."

"Can I grab a ride into town?"

"Flat tire on your bike?"

"Funny guy. No. I lent it to a…friend."

Ben pushed back his cap to see Johnny's face more clearly. "Yeah? What kind of friend?"

"A woman. No big deal. She came by for dinner and couldn't get a cab home."

Ben's smile was broad, his teeth very white. "What'd you do to scare her off?"

"Nothing. She left, that's all." He felt mildly uncomfortable that a woman leaving his house after dinner was seen as such a big deal. It happened, didn't it? As occurred so frequently between him and Ben, they had the same memory at the same time.

"Not another mental breakdown?"

"No. And Amber didn't have a mental breakdown. She was just sad."

"Sad is when you feel a little blue, maybe shed a few tears. That girl was sobbing so hard I swear tears were squirting out of her eyes. I've never seen anything like it." Johnny had called Ben in desperation when it was clear the woman he'd had fun with that evening was having a major meltdown. Ben and his truck were there within minutes.

"Thanks. I remember. She started crying the second we got here. Said I reminded her of her old boyfriend."

"The one who had a restraining order."

"Can we talk about something else?"

"Sure. How psycho was this one?"

"Not psycho at all. A bit old-fashioned, I guess."

Ben let out a low whistle. "No doing the dirty before marriage?"

"No. I don't think so. More like, not on a first date."

"She said that? She used the word *date?*"

Johnny nodded.

"She a Mormon or something?"

"I don't think so."

"Wow. It's good for you to get slapped down once in a while. You have it too easy. Ladies fall all over themselves for the hottie behind the bar. Makes me sick."

Johnny grinned at his old buddy. "You should have stayed in the hospitality business."

"Tell me about it. All I see all day is sweaty guys with meat hands." Nobody knew better than Johnny that Ben was only alone when he chose to be. If Ben partied harder and more seriously since the woman he was set to marry dumped him two weeks before the wedding, Johnny figured it was his own business. Ben reached over and helped himself to an orange quarter, sucking out the juice in one quick move. "What time do you need to be downtown?"

"I start work at four."

"Okay. I'll come get you around three-thirty and I can report on your building."

"Great."

"By the way, I'm going back into the restaurant biz. Hennington Lodge had some water damage in the restaurant. I'll be hanging out with your girlfriend, Rita."

"Tell her I'm working on my masterpiece. A martini so incredible it will change gin as we know it. My drink is like Prozac, Viagra and Vitamin E in one delicious mouthful."

Ben had taken another orange slice, now he stopped sucking, the orange quarter stuck to his mouth like a clown smile. He pulled the orange rind away and stared. "That true?"

"No. But that's what you can tell Rita."

He rose, stretching his long frame. "You're choking

under pressure. That's bad." He drained the last of his coffee and turned back toward the house. "That's very bad."

Johnny was not choking under pressure. Sure, he wanted his trophy back, and he was going to get it.

All he had to do was come up with a fresh, innovative cocktail, exactly as he'd done for a dozen years before Rita blew into town. He'd design another. And soon.

As soon as he came up with a fresh, innovative idea.

RITA HAD A CRICK in her neck. She was tired of looking up, but she couldn't help herself. Maybe if she stared hard enough and long enough, she'd will Ben to fall off the ladder he was perched on, his all-too-muscular physique displayed for all to see as he contorted himself around joists or whatever those hunks of lumber were in the ceiling.

Not that she wished him dead or anything, but a cleanly broken leg, neatly sprained wrist, something to keep him out of her way would be great about now.

It was late afternoon, before the restaurant opened for dinner, and after the last guests had lingered over lunch. The bar was nominally open, though there were only two customers, a couple still looking sweaty after a game of tennis, racquets leaning against their chairs as they sipped imported beers and, based on their hand gestures, replayed the game they'd just spent hours playing.

Steph, the lone cocktail waitress followed Rita's gaze up to where Ben was bent in something like a yoga pose, reaching forward, his jeans stretched tight over his hips.

"That's a prime cut of man meat right there."

Rita let out a snort of derision. "We should both go on a diet."

Steph glanced at her in mock horror. "As if." She kept her gaze on Ben's impressive overhead contortions. "I keep meaning to take him home one night, but I always seem to end up with somebody else." She turned back to Rita. "You ever sleep with him?"

Rita transferred her attention to the eager face gazing up. "Don't you ever think about anything but getting laid?"

"Sure I do." She grinned. "But not when I'm looking up at a guy's ass wondering what he looks like naked."

"The tennis players have empty glasses. Go see if they need another beer."

"Yes, grouchy boss."

"I'm not grouchy."

But she was. She knew it. The guy crawling around six feet above her head was the cause.

After about fifteen more minutes, when she'd spent a lot more time with her attention on him than on her work, he came down off the ladder. Above the tan work gloves his bare forearms were dark and nearly hairless. Muscles rippled on his upper arms and stretched the chest of the faded T-shirt. His baseball cap had sawdust on it.

"Stay away from my workstation with that crap all over you," she snapped.

His dark eyes snapped to hers. "What's wrong with you?"

"Nothing. I'm busy and I want you gone."

Ben stood there for a moment considering her. "You're not going to offer me a drink?"

She didn't raise her gaze from the limes she was cutting. "Staff room's in back of the kitchen. You can drink in there."

"You were staring at me the whole time I was up that ladder. Now you won't even look at me."

"Don't get excited. I was giving you the evil eye. I wanted you to fall off the ladder."

"You're a mental case, you know that?" He turned and with an aggressive snap, had the ladder down and ready to remove.

"This is a piddly little repair job. What's the big boss doing here?"

"You got a problem with me working in this hotel?"

She raised her head and glared at him. "Yeah. I do."

He glared right back. "Well, get used to it."

She would have cut herself, probably chopped off her whole finger if she hadn't already laid down the knife. "You mean you're doing this whole job yourself?"

"No. I'll probably have an assistant. Maybe two. It's not a huge job, but it's tricky. The rain's gotten in through a patch in the roof. Some of the joists are bordering on unstable. There's also a wiring issue that I want to get an electrician to inspect. And this inn is a good client of mine, so I want to do the job myself."

"I can't work in the middle of a construction zone."

He huffed an exaggerated sigh. "We'll do our best to keep the mess and noise to a minimum. If it wasn't a hotel, we'd start really early when you're not working, but I don't think the hotel guests would appreciate that, do you?"

"I'm sure you have more important jobs. Why don't you send in a foreman?"

His mouth twisted in a grin that a lot of women would probably find very sexy. "Maybe I just like being around you."

She was about to retort when Steph joined them, tray in hand. "Hey, Ben."

"How you doing?"

He must have met Stephanie half a dozen times. Rita bet he didn't even know her name.

"I'm fine." She flicked her long hair in a flirtatious manner. "Haven't seen you around the last couple of weeks."

"I've been busy."

"Well, me and my roommate are having some people over tonight. You should drop by."

Ben glanced from one woman to the other. "Maybe I will."

"Rita, the tennis players want Heineken refills."

"Sure."

She got the beers, opened them and poured them into long glasses while Steph wrote her address on her order pad. "I'll put my phone number here, too. In case you get lost—" she glanced up at him through her long lashes "—or anything."

"Thanks."

She ripped the paper from the pad and handed it to him, then picked up her tray and headed off to the table where her only customers sat.

Ben glanced at the paper in his hand. Folded it and put it in his pocket.

"Did she put her name on there?"

"Yeah. Stephanie." He raised his brows. "What, you think I didn't remember her name? I remembered."

"Sure you did, tiger."

"So, you going to this party?"

"Depends. You?"

He shrugged. "Depends."

8

Naked Lady

1 oz gin
1 oz vodka
7-Up to taste

Mix in a cocktail glass over ice.

NATALIE DRESSED with care and tried very hard to make it seem that she hadn't. Her jeans were the brand-new ones she'd got last time she was in New York and they were both tighter and lower cut than what she was used to. She suspected they'd been designed for those women who have a tattoo on their lower back, and a thong rising out of their pants.

She wore a belt to stop them slipping too low and a Marc Jacobs T-shirt that was long enough so that her lack of tattoos and thong would be a matter of speculation rather than obvious fact.

It wasn't that she went heavier on her makeup, she didn't, but she did use more products. Eyeliner as well as a barely there shadow. Two coats of mascara instead of one, a little liquid foundation with a touch of glimmer and lipstick as well as her usual swish of clear gloss.

Her hair was brushed until it gleamed and she wore it down so it swung past her shoulders. Of course, when she put Johnny's bike helmet on, the style was compromised, but she'd done her best.

The ride down to the restaurant took her less than five minutes. She thought she might eat her dinner up at the bar, in the manner of a daring single woman who had flings if she felt like it. Making sure not to order anything such as spinach that tended to get stuck in the teeth or garlic, she'd flirt with the bartender and let nature take its course.

That was her plan, anyway, but when she got there the parking lot was full, which suggested Johnny might not have a lot of time for flirting.

She leaned the bike against the wall of the restaurant, behind a tree where she prayed no one would be able to see it, then she scrambled in her bag for her brush, yanked off the helmet and brushed her hair before heading into the restaurant.

When she entered she discovered that the parking lot was full for a reason.

The whole place was packed. Including the bar, where every seat was occupied and eight people stood huddled in groups around the perimeter.

Disaster!

Johnny had his back to her, but when he turned around he looked exactly as laid-back as he always did. He traded comments with the guy whose drink he was serving, picked up an empty glass, and moved to where a waitress was standing ready to give an order.

"Do you have a reservation?" a friendly woman asked her.

"No. I came to drop something off for Johnny, but he looks busy."

As though he'd heard his name, which of course was impossible, he glanced up then and saw her. Giving her a friendly smile, he waved her over.

He walked around to the far edge of the bar to meet her.

"I brought your bike back, but I don't know where to park it."

"Where is it?"

"In the front. Behind a tree."

"Okay. Thanks." She handed him the helmet and he took it.

"Should I move it somewhere safer?"

"Naah, it'll be okay. I'll go lock it up when I get a chance."

"What if it gets stolen in the meantime?"

He seemed puzzled by the question. "Everybody local knows my bike. If some bike thief is passing through town and wants it badly enough, I guess they'll take it."

"I could lock it up for you if you have a lock."

But he was already turning back to his busy drink kingdom. "Don't worry about it."

"Okay." She stood there for another second. He was busy. There was no room for her to sit and eat dinner. She felt deflated. An extra customer he didn't have time for.

She said, "See you."

"Yeah, see you."

She headed out of the restaurant and, not knowing what else to do, saw a cab letting off passengers and asked the driver if he was available.

"Am now. Hop in."

She slid into the back.

"Where to?"

"A restaurant. Where can you recommend that has good food where I won't feel conspicuous eating alone?"

"Price an obstacle?" he asked, meeting her gaze in the rearview mirror. He reminded her of her Uncle Matt. Same puppy-dog-brown eyes and balding head.

"No," she said, grateful not for the first time for her generous expense account.

"The Hennington Lodge. Great food. Quiet atmosphere. Nobody cares if you're alone and it's not some pickup joint, if you know what I mean. People will respect your privacy."

The Hennington. Where she was staying. Where she'd left. Instead of a nice evening chatting with her cute bartender and possible fling, she'd be eating alone and everyone would respect her privacy. "Sounds good."

When she walked into the hotel dining room, as she'd half suspected, she found Rita behind the bar.

There was one seat empty. She climbed on it and received a smile from the bartender.

"What can I get you?"

"Is it okay if I eat dinner here at the bar? I really don't feel like sitting at a table by myself." She did it all the time, but for some reason tonight wasn't turning out the way she'd hoped and the idea of a solo table wasn't appealing.

"Sure. I'm in a bad mood. I'll be glad of the company."

"Your table is ready, sir," a woman said and the

couple beside Natalie left, without hearing Rita's next words she fervently hoped.

"So, how's Operation Hot Johnny coming?"

"It's not. I took his bike back just now, but the place was so busy I couldn't get near him. I can't keep showing up at the restaurant, I'll feel like a stalker."

Rita considered for a moment. "You know where he lives. You could put yourself naked in his bed."

"How would I get in?"

"He has a hidden key. I know where it is."

"You know where Johnny hides his key?"

"Most everybody does. Half the time he leaves the patio door open anyway. You won't have any trouble getting in."

"And how would I feel if he showed up with another woman?"

"You into threesomes?"

Natalie let her horrified expression answer for her.

"Then, awkward."

She sighed. "Face it, it's hopeless. I had my chance to fulfill my wildest fantasy—" She stopped when she saw Rita's expression. "Okay, so I'm not very wild. For me, sleeping with a strange bartender is about as wild as it gets." She sighed. "I had my chance and I didn't take it."

"I've known a lot of men in my time. Most of them, what they can't have, they want even more."

"Sure didn't seem that way tonight."

"Trust me."

Rita retrieved a bottle of Bordeaux for one waitress, prepared three mixed cocktails for a huffy-looking waiter, one of which looked like a Cosmopolitan, possibly the only mixed drink Natalie felt she could identify on sight.

Then she took Natalie's order for a glass of white wine and some fancy salad with goat cheese and candied pecans that sounded appealing.

When she placed the glass in front of Natalie, she seemed to have a lull.

"So, what about you?" Natalie asked her. "We always talk about me, but I don't know anything about you. Are you with anyone?"

"I don't believe in getting tied down to one man. Life's too short, you know?"

Natalie sipped her wine. "Sometimes I feel like I am the last person on the planet who still believes in true love."

"Oh, don't let my cynicism ruin your day. I'm in a bad mood. Thing is, we probably all get what we believe we'll get. You'll have true love and I'll never settle."

"Well," Natalie said, raising her glass in a mock toast, "here's to getting what you want."

A waitress with long, curly red hair, so curly it looked like thin birthday-present ribbon that had been scraped by scissors, came up and sagged against the bar. "My feet hurt."

"Steph, I keep telling you, if you're going to wear those stilettos, your feet are always going to hurt."

Steph picked up her foot and contemplated the four-inch black strappy heels. "I know. But I get the best tips when I wear them." She grinned at Natalie. "They make my legs look killer."

Natalie looked down and she had to admit she was looking at killer legs. They were long like a dancer's, and muscular.

"Wow. Are you a dancer?"

"Thanks. I danced ballet when I was little, but the bod's from surfing. It's a great workout." Natalie took one look at the killer bod in the short black dress and decided she was going to take up surfing. Steph then transferred her attention to Rita. "I need two margaritas on rocks, one with no salt, a Courvoisier and a B&B."

"You got it. Hey, Steph, is it okay if I bring Natalie here to your party tonight?"

"Sure. The more the merrier." Then she turned so her hair danced around her head. "I thought you weren't coming."

"I never said I wasn't coming. I said I might."

"Yeah, but when you say you might, you never show."

"Not this time."

"Cool."

When she was out of earshot, Rita leaned forward like a woman with a secret. "Stephanie's roommate Troy works in the Driftwood with Johnny. He'll probably be at their party tonight."

"But—" her head was in a whirl "—I can't go partying to pick up guys. I've got to work tomorrow."

Rita shrugged. "It's up to you. Then don't come whining to me that you can't get a guy in your bed if you're not willing to put in any effort."

Natalie stabbed a pecan and it split in two. "Are you positive he'll be there?"

"No."

"Where is this party?"

"I'll take you."

"But—"

"Go home. Grab a nap. Come back here at two."

"I can't believe I'm even considering going to a party that doesn't start until two o'clock in the morning," she groused. But even she could hear the excitement in her voice.

9

After Party

2 cups vodka
4 cups cranberry juice
2 qt ginger ale
4 cups pineapple juice
1 cup orange juice
Simple sugar syrup to taste

Mix in a punch bowl.

JOHNNY WAS ALMOST finished cleaning the bar when Ben hailed him.

He looked up and saw that his old friend was wearing a white shirt that looked suspiciously ironed and a clean pair of jeans. "If you came to give me the estimate on the work for the apartment building, I can wait until tomorrow."

"Naah. I'm going to this party some girl at the Hennington is throwing. Her name's Stephanie. I figured you'd be going. Came by to give you a ride."

"You know, Stephanie's a real nice girl, but she's got the IQ of a loaf of bread."

"Who says I'm looking for an intelligent conversation? Hell, who says I'm looking for anything?"

Johnny sniffed loudly. "I smell aftershave."

"So, I'm not a pig like you. You want a ride or don't you?"

"What if you get lucky? How'm I going to get home?"

"You can take my truck."

"Okay."

"I'll throw your bike in the back. See you out front."

Ben's truck, which was ridiculously large, sported the company logo on the side. Johnny had pretty much stopped hassling Ben about it. He had, however, signed Ben up for several online green newsletters.

Ben muscled the truck up the steep street leading to the rancher that Troy and Stephanie shared.

An assortment of vehicles suggested the party was in full swing when Ben and Johnny arrived with a case of beer.

The front door of the house opened into the kitchen, and when they stepped inside, Stephanie glanced up and giggled. "Hey, you made it."

Since this remark was obviously addressed to Ben, Johnny didn't feel obliged to answer. Instead, he put the beer into the big bucket of ice the hosts had provided and then, grabbing one for himself and handing another to Ben, he walked into the main room. Pretty much everyone here he knew. He nodded, said hello to a few people, got hugged by a woman he thought was a massage therapist in town, and kept heading toward the open doors onto the back deck.

Rita was standing with her back against the rail facing his way. He registered slight surprise. She didn't usually party with the rest of the staff. She looked red-hot, too, in a skimpy black skirt, a silky-looking white top and do-me heels. A woman was talking to her;

from her back he didn't think he knew her. Slim, with curly brown hair. Tight jeans. Nice ass.

Rita glanced over as he stepped out onto the deck, nodded, then looked past him. "Well, well. Look what the cat dragged in."

He didn't realize Ben had followed him until he spoke.

"Rita. Didn't know you'd be here."

"I'm full of surprises. I don't think you've met my friend Natalie."

At that moment, the woman with the long brown hair turned her head.

"Natalie?" he said, sounding like a dork.

She seemed a little flustered to see him. She reached up and flipped her hair over her shoulder with one hand. He thought she might be blushing but it was hard to tell with only candles lighting the patio. "Hi, Johnny."

"Hi. Good to see you." And it was.

He stepped closer to her. "It was so busy I didn't get a chance to talk to you before."

"It was busy." She sipped from a sparkling drink that seemed to be some fancy water.

"So, how do you know Rita?"

"I'm staying at the lodge—that's my client, actually—so I've got to know her. She invited me to come tonight. She's a lot of fun."

He glanced away and found Rita still giving Ben a hard time about something. Then Rita said, "Later," and headed off as Ben watched her.

Ben getting blown off by a gorgeous woman was an interesting spectacle, but not as interesting as the woman standing in front of him. "Pretty late for you to be partying. Don't you have to get up early for work?"

She shrugged. "I had a nap earlier. I'm doing okay."

A couple moved from the wicker two-seater and he motioned with his hand. "Do you want to sit down?"

"Sure."

She settled herself, turning her body slightly so she was facing him. Their knees brushed and she didn't move away. It was oddly intimate out here in the candlelight, while the noise and action of the party took place inside.

"I was surprised when I saw you standing there."

She sent him a quizzical look from under her eyelashes. "I hope it was a good surprise?"

"Definitely."

He shifted so they were touching thigh to thigh. Once more she didn't move away. He liked the warmth they were generating, the way her hair drifted around her face as the breeze played with it. He reached out, wanting to touch it, too. The strands were soft against his fingers. "I like your hair down like this. It's sexy."

"Thanks."

"You're welcome."

They were quiet for a bit. He didn't feel like getting into a big conversation and got the feeling she didn't, either.

"It's a nice night," she said.

"Mmm."

"I bet it would look gorgeous from your patio."

He turned to study her face. "Are you saying what I think you're saying?"

"That I'd like to come home with you? Yes." She looked a little astonished by her own boldness and then added, "Unless you want to stay here, which I would totally understand."

"No. I don't really feel like partying. Let's go back to my place." He suddenly recalled their conversation last night when she'd backed off. "If you're sure you want to."

She nodded. "I'm sure."

"Great." He took her hand and hauled her to her feet.

"Um, how will we get there? I don't think it would be safe for both of us on your bike."

"It's okay. I'll borrow Ben's truck. The guy you almost just met. He owes me."

He found Ben talking to the massage therapist. Since they were talking about rock climbing, he didn't feel too bad interrupting. "Hey, Ben, I'm heading out. I promised Natalie a ride. Okay if I take your truck?"

Ben hesitated. Looked around the kitchen as though trying to decide if there was anyone else he needed to talk to, seemed to decide there wasn't and said, "It's okay. I'm ready to go. I'll drive you home."

"Thanks."

He said goodbye to the few people in the vicinity.

Natalie crossed the room to take leave of Rita, who was mixing drinks, as if she didn't get enough of that at the lodge. He studied her for a moment, one master observing another. She was smooth, well practiced. And he liked her style. Of course, he'd like it even more once he got his trophy back from her. Which reminded him, he had to get started on his prizewinning drink. The competition was next week.

When the three of them piled into Ben's truck, Natalie ended up sandwiched between him and Ben. After sizing up Ben as though she was considering giving him a Breathalyzer test before getting into his truck, she obviously decided that one beer hadn't made him too drunk to drive and slid in.

"You didn't stay long," he said, wondering why Ben had been so eager to go if he didn't plan to stay.

"Long enough."

Whatever.

The road hugged the shore, a ride he loved on his bike at night, but the truck was definitely a lot faster. And with Natalie beside him, he didn't want to waste any time.

"Thanks, Ben," he said when they pulled up outside his place.

"Thanks," Natalie said, sounding a little shy. "It was nice meeting you."

"Yeah. You, too."

He unloaded his bike out of the back and then turned to see Ben head back to the road. He was continuing on to his house rather than back to the party. Maybe Stephanie was too much of an airhead after all.

Probably it was a good thing Ben was going home alone. He'd been partying way too hard. Though, now Johnny came to think of it, not recently.

Well, that was a puzzle for another day.

Natalie was waiting.

He pushed the bike into the garage, then, taking her hand, walked around to the front, where the deck looked over the sea. He heard her breathe in deeply. "I love it here," she said.

"It's a special place."

She shivered and he stepped behind her, putting his arms around her, pulling her against him. She was lithe and supple. Not a hard body, by any means, but soft, womanly.

He held her like that for a while, his chin just resting on the top of her head, breathing in the scent of the ocean, and of her.

After a bit she turned and lifted her face in mute invitation. Which he took immediate advantage of, bending to kiss her. Her lips were cool, a little salty, and when he pulled her in closer, she slid her arms up around his neck, kissing him back with full passion and none of the hesitance she'd shown last night. She'd clearly made her peace with whatever had held her back.

Making him a very happy man.

"Let's go inside," she whispered.

He didn't speak, merely took her hand and led her inside, through the darkened main room to his bedroom. As always on preparing for bed, the first thing he did was open the French doors.

He heard her disappear into the bathroom, and took the time to turn down the bed, yank a few condoms out of his bedside table and place them discreetly beside the lamp base where he could find them easily.

He slipped off his shoes and socks, then, when she emerged, he took his own turn in the bathroom. He brushed his teeth fast, wished he had time to shave, but the thought of her out there waiting for him made him restless. There was something about her that was elusive. She'd already changed her mind once. He didn't want her changing it back again, not when he was as worked up as he was.

He reentered the bedroom and she was standing at the window; he wasn't sure if she was drawn to be as near the water as possible, or if she was contemplating bolting.

"Nice night," he said as he crossed the room in his bare feet.

"Very," she said, turning, and in her expression he saw a mixture of shyness and eagerness, but no hint that she was about to borrow his bike again.

"You know, you have a great mouth," he said, kissing it thoroughly.

"My lips aren't very big."

"Not too big and not too small." He kissed her again. "Just right."

While they were kissing, he slipped his hands under the hem of her shirt. Her skin was warm and silky. He felt his own blood start to heat as his hands trailed up, to the breasts he'd touched last night and wanted more of.

He'd planned to go so slowly, but he felt a heat coming off this woman, and a need that was communicating itself to him at some basic level. He dragged her shirt up, breaking contact with her mouth only long enough to get the damn thing over her head and off.

He had her bra unsnapped and sailing into the corner of the room, and then he paused to gaze at her.

"You are beautiful," he said.

"No," she giggled, as though the idea were ridiculous. But she was. Her neck was long, her shoulders elegant and her breasts high and firm. The long lines of her stomach ended at the low-slung waistband of her jeans.

She reached for his shirt and he helped her take it off, then pulled her close again, enjoying the rub of her skin against his, the feel of her heart beating.

When she connected a line of soft kisses from one side of his chest to the other, she almost undid him. He pushed her back on the bed, toppling her so she fell laughing onto the mattress. He traced the waistband of her jeans with one finger that wasn't quite steady, then unsnapped and unzipped her. Her gaze stayed on his as she raised her hips so he could drag her jeans and panties off in one not completely smooth movement.

He was even less coordinated when he yanked the last of his own clothes off. He was too eager. It was ridiculous. But he felt as if he was going to go off like a firecracker and embarrass himself.

He needed to distract himself. Other men might recite the presidents or set themselves math problems. Johnny tested himself on obscure drink recipes.

When he kissed her and the taste and scent of her had his temperature climbing too fast, he mentally prepared a Pink Lady. Not a drink asked for too often, but Natalie's pink-tipped nipples against her white skin made him think of a pink lady.

He licked her nipples and she gasped, her back rising off the bed.

Interesting. Every female body was a brand-new puzzle, he found. Part of the pleasure was in discovering a woman's particular hot spots. With Natalie, the nipples were extrasensitive. He took his time, licking gently; loving the way her skin puckered and shifted under his tongue.

They were so sensitive he was careful to suck on her with only the most gentle suction and his reward was in her sighed, "Oh, yes."

He decided that if he could concoct a drink that tasted like this, he'd have his trophy back permanently.

10

Pink Lady

1 oz gin
1 tsp grenadine
1 tsp light cream

Shake with ice. Strain into a cocktail glass.

NATALIE HAD NEVER THOUGHT of the male body as anything to get too excited about, but she realized, seeing Johnny naked, that she had never before studied the greatest specimens, so it wasn't fair to judge.

Johnny was, in a word, gorgeous. He wasn't huge with bulky muscles, but all that surfing and sailing and bike riding had given him definition. His chest was broad, his belly striated with muscle so he looked like the guys on the cover of *Men's Health*. Even his butt was cute. Round and hard, so she couldn't resist sliding her palm over his cheeks.

And his penis! She sneaked a peek, and then another. It wasn't huge or anything, but she was beginning to think Frederick had been shortchanged in that department. And therefore, for several years of her life, so had she.

Natalie had never thought of herself as particularly passionate or greedy in bed, but tonight she felt both. She wanted it all. She wanted to try everything she'd ever dreamed of, every passionate, crazy, forbidden fantasy she'd ever imagined.

Johnny, she suspected, was exactly the man to help her try anything she had a mind to.

His hands were all over her. Johnny touched her as though he loved the feel of her. As though she were new and special and something to be savored.

When he'd kissed her mouth for so long she grew light-headed, he moved south. Kissing her chin, her throat and her chest. He spent a long time on her breasts, kissing and sucking them. At first, she'd braced herself. A lot of men seemed to think that nipples were for yanking, biting and twisting. But hers were so sensitive, they wanted a gentle touch. Johnny got it immediately, giving her soft attention that had her body pulsing with need in no time, building heat within her. He dragged his nose between them making her giggle.

"You smell fantastic," he said.

"You're reacting to my pheromones."

"Never heard them called that before," he said, squeezing her breasts gently.

"Very funny. Pheromones are chemicals we give off. Every person's scent is completely original to them and contains elements of their immune system. Did you know that a big part of sexual attraction is finding someone whose immune system is completely different from yours? That ensures healthy children. At least, that's what I've read."

"That's interesting."

He kissed her, just below her breasts, in an area she'd

never known was so sensitive. "Sorry. I get carried away."

"No. It's good. I love the way you talk smart in bed. Tell me something else. I need things to concentrate on so I don't make a fool of myself and come before I'm ready."

Her smile bloomed bigger than a sunflower. "I do that to you?"

"Uh, yeah."

"Let me see." His excitement ramped up hers and gave her the courage to reach down and touch him. She found him iron hard and as her fingers reached around him and gently squeezed, he closed his eyes and groaned.

"You'll kill me. I'll keel over right here and die and my obituary will read Coitus Croaks Bartender. And I haven't even had the coitus part yet."

"No, don't die. Not before we finish. Promise me."

He pulled her hand away, kissed it. Smiled up at her from his wicked blue eyes. "Promise."

"Let's get you ready."

From the way she was feeling, so hot it was like an ache, she didn't think she could stand to be touched. "I think I am ready," she whispered, as he reached between her legs. She gasped, her body arching up against his questing fingers.

"Wow. Are you ever ready."

She tried to hold on to sanity long enough to remind him of the importance of protection, but he was already reaching for the night table and she relaxed, knowing he'd already prepared.

The sound of the tearing condom wrapper was like a hit of aphrodisiac to her brain. He'd worried about embarrassing himself, but she was very much afraid she was the one who was about to have a premature orgasm. But her body didn't seem to care if it gave her away as a woman who hadn't had sex in far too long and what she'd had, had been mediocre at best. Instinctively, she and her pheromones knew they had something special going on here. She couldn't hold her hips still. It was embarrassing, as if they had their own agenda.

In a second he was ready, and she opened for him as he pushed slowly inside her.

The slow friction was torture. She was right on the edge, and needed so little to go off like a rocket. And so she grabbed at his butt, squeezing his cheeks in her need, pulling him down into her, even as she thrust up against him.

"Oh, baby, I can't," he groaned, but she barely heard him. She was exploding, gripping and grabbing at him as they surged and bucked against each other, hard and strong and needy.

She heard her own cry, imagined it floating out the window and sailing across the ocean. The orgasm that had been building for years.

With a huge groan, he followed her, stretching the incredible sensations out with a few long, slow strokes that left him shuddering until he fell limply on top of her.

She heard the air rasping in his throat, and when he turned onto his back, pulling her with him, she heard his heart hammer beneath her ear.

When he could talk again he said, "I'm usually a little smoother than that."

"Yeah? Prove it."

"What?" He turned his head to look at her.

She felt completely wonderful and a little full of herself. "You going somewhere?" She raised herself, kissed him lightly. "I said, prove how smooth you can be." Then she grinned. "We've got all night."

"Uh-huh." He was sweaty, his face a little flushed from exertion, and she'd been right about him when she first met him. If there was a place this guy looked most at home, it wasn't behind the bar or reefing a sail or dancing on a surfboard, though all those things were part of him.

Where he looked most as if he was doing what he was born to do best, was right here, in a rumpled bed, burning up the sheets.

She propped herself up on one elbow, grinning down at him. "And there are some things I've always wanted to try." She'd be gone in a week and she'd never see Johnny again. They moved in entirely difference circles in completely different parts of the country. Which meant that here was the perfect opportunity for her to explore all those things she'd read about furtively in certain magazines, the ones that had quizzes with titles like, "Are You a Tiger in the Bedroom?" The only tests in her life that she'd ever failed.

But if there was ever a guy who could turn a tame woman into a tiger in the bedroom, on the sand, the kitchen counter, and any other conceivable surface or location, she was pretty sure Johnny was that man.

He'd started looking a little sleepy, however, at her words, he started nibbling on her bare shoulder. "What things have you always wanted to try?"

"Well, I think maybe…" She cleared her throat. What kind of an idiot said they wanted to try new things after sleeping with a guy for the first time? Who knew what sort of kinky things he might be into? For her, wild and crazy would be sex in a place other than a Posturepedic bed. "Oh, never mind."

"No, you've got me intrigued. What things have you always wanted to try?"

He continued caressing her as he talked and she realized that what she'd always wanted to try was someone like him. Who wasn't caught up in business and efficiency, who thought it was fun to try new things in bed. "Nothing too wild."

"Give me some hints. Are we talking barnyard animals?"

"Eew. Of course not."

"The cast of the Rockettes?"

"Like I need competition."

"Trapeze equipment?"

There was a pause during which she heard the pound of the surf through the open door. "What sort of trapeze equipment?"

He laughed softly, and she felt the puff of breath against her breast. "You're a wild woman underneath that business suit facade, aren't you?"

Her mouth twisted in a wry smile. "No. I only wish I were."

"Hey, I'm fine with the good old basics," he said, moving south, kissing her belly. "Why don't we start with those and see where it goes from there?"

As she grew heavy with renewed desire, she pretty much thought she was happy with the basics, too.

RITA WAS NOT HAVING the greatest night of her life. What was she even doing at this party? She tended bar for her regular job and here she was playing bartender at a house party. Not that anyone had asked her, she somehow started mixing drinks.

Now it was four in the morning; somebody was smoking, which she hated; half the people here were too drunk to drive, or were already asleep on floors, couches, heaven knew where. As usual, the hard-core partiers had migrated to the kitchen, sitting around the table telling war stories.

Stephanie hadn't mourned Ben's early departure too long, she noted. She was sitting on the lap of Gord, one of the chefs at the Driftwood, who was rubbing her back in a way that suggested he'd be cooking her breakfast in the morning.

She hadn't even intended to come. Had no idea why she'd bothered.

Except she had.

Well, she was too young to be den mother to a bunch of hospitality workers. Luckily, Steph and her roommate Troy were among the soberest people here. She thought she'd better make her exit before the young woman gave up her hostess duties and took her cook to bed.

"Steph? You're confiscating car keys, right? Nobody drives if they've been drinking."

"Yep. Me and Troy are on patrol." She got off Gord's lap, giving him a pat and came closer to Rita. Her pretty mouth turned down. "This is not how I thought my night would end." She glanced up at Rita. "I totally thought the cute carpenter was mine. I heard he's fantastic in bed. But do I get to try him out?" She threw her hands in the air. "No. I didn't even see him leave. I bet he left with Tracy. She's been talking about hooking up with him, too."

"Huh. Well, Gord's got the look in his eyes. He'll take good care of you tonight. It was a great party. But I've got to get going."

Steph, true to her promise, looked at Rita carefully. "You fit to drive?"

"Yeah. I was so busy slinging drinks I didn't have time to drink one."

In truth, she hadn't been feeling like drinking lately. Maybe it was working around booze all day. She was drinking less all the time. Soon she'd be the Teetotal Bartender. She'd poured Natalie and herself sparkling water when they first arrived and then had a refill later on, after Natalie left on Johnny's arm, looking more bubbly than the Perrier.

"Well, thanks for coming." Steph reached over and gave her a borderline sloppy hug. "We should hang out more."

"Sure. We hardly ever see each other what with working in the same place and all."

Steph looked at her as if maybe she'd made a joke, but it was hard to tell. "Right. Well, see you tomorrow."

Rita raised a hand in the general direction of the table. "Night."

She got into her car, started the engine. She tapped her long, bronze-painted fingernails against the steering wheel for a minute, then turned, not left, the direction of her apartment, but right.

She knew the road so well she didn't even have to think about the route, but drove on autopilot, letting Sufjan Stevens belt out of the speakers as she drove.

The house was dark when she arrived. She pulled into the driveway, all the way in to the empty garage where no one would see her car from the road. It was their signal. If he had company, he parked in the garage and she would know to drive on. But his truck was out in the open, the garage as empty as she felt.

She killed the engine. Grabbed her workout bag from the backseat, and found the key that was always under the third rock beneath the window.

Once the door was unlocked, she slipped the key back into its place and let herself quietly into the sleeping house.

A low whine and the thump of a tail against the wall told her that in fact she wasn't the only one awake. "Hey, Buddy, how you doing?"

She squatted and let the big dog lick her face. Even though it was dark, she knew he was sitting in the classic, "If I sit, do I get a treat?" pose he'd perfected.

She opened the flap of her purse and extracted the foil doggy bag containing the pieces of tenderloin that a diner hadn't finished. If Buddy's tail had been wagging before, it was now going at warp speed. He was a big Lab, but a delicate eater, and as greedy as he was for the beef, he didn't take off half her hand or slobber all over her. He took the meat delicately with his teeth, and then she heard him chomp and smack, whining with greedy pleasure, before he took the other piece.

"It's our little secret," she said, giving him another pat before standing and disposing of the doggie bag in the kitchen trash.

She slipped down the hall to the bathroom, stripped naked, washed, brushed her teeth and padded down the hall knowing her way in the familiar house.

When she walked into the bedroom, even though it was dark, she knew he was there. His breathing was soft and slow, and she could smell him. She closed her eyes for a second, breathing him in, then walked the rest of the way across the room and slipped into bed.

When she wrapped herself around him she found him also naked and warm from sleep. She kissed his chest first, then his belly, trailing her tongue down his buff, smooth body. By the time she took him into her mouth, he was already hard. He'd woken and not made a sound or said a word.

As she pulled him into her mouth, he reached for her, rubbing her clit in time to her motions.

She licked and sucked at him for a while, making sure he had a good head of steam going, enjoying the heat building in her own body.

Then she climbed to her knees and straddled him, grasping his hard, wet cock and rubbing it against her entrance, then slowly lowering herself onto him.

Oh, how good he felt. She took him all the way into her and stilled for a moment, savoring the pleasure of having him inside her body, the feel of him filling her. His hands reached up to cover her heavy breasts.

"I expected you earlier," he said softly.

"I never want to be predictable." She knew he smiled in the dark, felt her own lips curve. Then she started to move and neither of them spoke.

She set the pace exactly as she liked it, changing the angle of her hips a little to increase her own pleasure, until she drove herself up to the first peak and over, tipping her head back as the force of her climax shook her.

She'd barely caught her breath before she found herself being pushed backward as he rose to meet her, so they were face-to-face, legs crossed over each

other's, positioned like the lovers in those old porno-
graphic Japanese woodcuts.

She came again, bucking against him, her body
already slick with sweat. They were both breathing
hard. She collapsed onto her back and he finished them
both off that way. Coming together in some mysterious way that mostly always worked for them.

She clung to him during the final moments of their
mating, and he dipped his head and kissed her, the first
time they'd kissed since she arrived.

They stayed tangled up, their harsh breathing filling
the room. When they'd cooled down, she rested her
palm lightly on the back of his hand where it was curled
around her breast. "Steph was sorry you left so early.
I think she had plans for you tonight."

"I had plans of my own."

"She said she heard you were fantastic in bed."

There was a moment's tense silence. "Did you think
I was a virgin when we met?" he asked.

"Naah. I thought you'd be flattered that the women
talk about you like that. Everyone knows you're a player."

He was stroking her, long, soothing movements of his
hand down her breast, her side, her hip and back up again.

Three orgasms and she was starting to get hot again.
Which only irritated her.

"The only person I've been playing with lately, is
you."

She turned her head, even though she could barely
see him. "I don't ask for anything, you know that.
You're free. And so am I. Hook up with anyone you
want to. If your truck's parked in your garage, I keep
going. It's a simple arrangement."

"Then how come you're pissed?"

11

Cola Rita

2 oz good quality tequila
2 oz triple sec
12 oz cola

Shake ingredients in a cocktail shaker with ice.
Strain into a highball glass.

"I'M NOT." She stretched out languidly, giving him
access to all of her that he wanted to touch, and Ben
wondered if he'd misheard the tone in her voice, but
he didn't think he had. "That's the beauty of this arrangement," she continued. "I am your basic wet
dream. I drop by when it suits us both. I'm gone when
you wake up. Nobody knows. It'll end when it ends.
No hearts broken, no feelings hurt."

Then why was he feeling that this was far from
perfect? They'd hooked up over a month ago. Johnny
had dragged him to an industry Scotch-tasting event,
knowing he liked a good Scotch, and somehow he and
Rita had ended up talking. First about Scotch, then
about a lot of stuff.

Both a little drunk, they'd shared one of the only

cabs in town. He'd suggested they drop her off first since her place was closer. They were side by side in the back of the cab, their thighs touching. She'd given him that cool, tough-girl look that got him every time, and said, "Why don't we just go straight to your place."

Before he'd managed to get his tongue around an enthusiastic yes, she'd kissed him. The power they ignited when their mouths met had pretty much flattened him.

She'd pulled back, staring at his mouth in astonishment, said, "Wow," and then he'd plastered his mouth against hers.

Only a desire not to get arrested made him pull away and try to talk like a normal person instead of an overgrown hormone until they arrived at his place.

They never got close to his bedroom. They'd done it up against the wall in his front hallway, her short black skirt hiked up to her hips, his jeans down around his ass.

They'd made love all evening and well into the night, by which time they'd sobered up and he'd driven her home.

He'd called her the next day at work and instead of accepting his dinner invitation, she said she'd drop by after work. After the fourth night, she'd suggested they needed a signal, so that if he was entertaining someone else, she'd know to drive on.

At the time he'd thought she was the coolest woman he'd ever met. Not sentimental, didn't want anything permanent. For a guy who spent a lot of time making sure no woman wanted more of him than he could give, it was a relief and a joy to have a woman in his life who wanted less than he was willing to give.

She didn't want romantic walks on the beach, nice dinners out, glasses of wine by the fire. She didn't want flowers or promises or long talks about their feelings, or where he thought the relationship was going.

She didn't even want to sleep in his bed a full night.

In fact, it soon became clear that she didn't want anyone knowing about them. At first it had been fun. A crazy secret they both shared that made waiting for her each night a kind of foreplay, the sex more potent than anything he'd ever experienced. She was like the hottest dream, and she visited him every single night.

So why, when it was going so well, did he suddenly feel as though he was being used?

She lay beside him. They'd developed a pattern where they did the wild and hot thing, then usually talked for a bit. Sometimes they fell into round two, sometimes not. And then she left.

It had been okay until today when she'd freaked out about him working at her restaurant, when she'd pointedly ignored him at the party.

But she'd gone to that party.

She never would have been there if he hadn't made a point of accepting the other girl's invite; that much he got.

He reached over, to where he kept water and glasses beside the condoms on the bedside table. And switched on the light.

Rita made a strangled sound and stuck her arm over her eyes. "You could have warned me. You almost blinded me."

"Sorry." He poured her some water. Handed it to her, nudging her wrist with the glass so she'd know it was there. She took it without comment. Then he poured himself a glass.

"Turn out the light."

"No. I want to see you. It's like you're two different women, the one who comes here at night, who I can only be with when it's dark, and the daytime Rita, who treats me like shit."

She took her arm from across her eyes and blinked a few times, then sipped from her water. If he'd expected an apology for the bitchy way she'd acted earlier, he was in for disappointment. He could tell the moment her eyes got used to the light that they were hard and snapping. "What do you want from me?"

"I—"

She rolled so she was propped on one elbow, her gorgeous dark skin gleaming in the light, her breasts canting to the side, making him want to bury his face between them. "What? You want to go out with me? You want me to be your *girlfriend?* Is that what you want?"

"I want to be more than a convenience fuck every night."

She laughed, a sudden laugh without much humor in it. "Do you think I'm joining that long list of yours?"

"What list?" He felt hot inside, as if he was angry, but he really didn't understand what he was angry about. Or why he was rocking this boat.

"The list of all the women you've been with since I first moved here? You hook up with these women, sometimes for a night, sometimes a few weeks. And then you're done."

"I never lie to any of those women. I'm always honest."

"I realize that. It's part of your rep. The women talk about how great you are in bed, and how you are incapable of commitment."

"It's not—"

"I'm honest, too." She took her hand and put it over his heart. Her hand was warm, not particularly soft. They were working hands. "This is as honest as I can be. If I hadn't been drunk that first time I never would have gone home with you. I don't want to be some woman you screwed and got tired of."

She suddenly flopped onto her back, and the water splashed against her glass. "What am I talking about? I am that woman. But when it happens, when you get tired of me—" she glared at him "—or I get tired of you, I don't want to be the latest hot gossip in Orca Bay. I don't want people asking me if I'm okay, and checking to see how we are with each other when we happen to be in the same room. I need to keep this—" here she gestured to the bed and the two of them naked in it "—separate from my daily life. It's the only way I can sleep with you and still face myself in the mirror every day."

"Can't we have dinner sometimes? Or go to a movie or something?"

"No. No dating. And no blabbing. Those are my terms. If you don't want to do that anymore, then this thing is over."

"What do you mean, no blabbing? You think I'd boast about my conquests? Some opinion you have of me."

She sighed. "I have a higher opinion of you than you understand." She touched his arm lightly. "Look, you know what this town is like. Everybody talks about everybody else. I wasn't here when your engagement broke up, but I've heard about it."

Even hearing her mention those words sent a cold jab through his gut. And the thought of all those morons down at the restaurant having nothing better to do than talk about his pathetic past was enough to make him want to hit something. "Heard what?"

"That you were different before. And after she left you, you weren't the same guy anymore."

"I grew up, that's all."

"I hope one day you get over her. Because you are better than this."

"I am over her."

"No. You're not. You punish every woman you can. Oh, you don't mean to. But you sleep with them and then you leave them. It's classic."

"What about you?" He made the same gesture to the two of them in the bed that she had earlier. "Am I punishing you?"

Her laugh was low and sent a chill through him. "No. See, I'm cynical, too."

He'd never thought about Rita's life before she came to Orca Bay. People came and went, it was that sort of place. You didn't spend a lot of time wondering who they were before they got here, or what had happened to them. But with Rita, he wanted to hear her story.

"So, what happened? To make you so cynical."

"You really want to know?"

He nodded.

She put her water on the table by the bed, reached behind her and stacked the pillows at her back. Then she crossed her arms under her naked breasts and said, "You tell me your story, I'll tell you mine."

Six weeks. Close to six weeks they'd been doing this nightly drop-by sex visit and he'd always managed to avoid the intimate talk that he hated. To his horror, he was the one initiating talking. Now that he'd asked to hear her story, she wanted to hear his. He should have kept his mouth shut.

"My story sucks."

"It's my deal. If you want my story you have to tell me yours first."

"I don't punish women!"

"Okay."

She waited.

Finally he sighed, shoved a pillow behind his back, so they were side by side, hips touching, and he told her. He hadn't told anyone, not even Johnny, the entire story.

"Her name was Sarah." He stopped and glanced at her. "Your turn."

"You mean we're not doing 'you tell your story, then I tell mine'?"

"No. We're telling them at the same time."

"And we're doing this line by line?"

"Yep."

She shook her head, amusement showing. "You're crazy. I'm sleeping with a crazy man." He simply stared at her with his mouth shut until she snapped, "Fine. His name was Jeff."

"We met in college. She was a finance major. Turned out our fathers knew each other and they completely approved of us." He stopped, letting Rita know it was her turn.

"Jeff was my roommate's boyfriend's best friend. He wanted to be a doctor. I thought he was so smart, and caring and I was flattered when he chose me."

"We went out all through college. I wanted to marry Sarah. I talked it over with my dad, and then asked her father if I could marry her." He made a sound of derision. "Old fashioned crap, I know, but her family was very traditional Chinese. And I loved her. I honored her. We got engaged after we graduated. She got a job at a top finance firm in San Francisco." He stopped. Swallowed, seeing himself as so young, so naive. How little he'd known about women. He nudged Rita with his elbow, indicating it was her turn to talk.

"When my roommate moved in with her boyfriend it seemed the easiest thing for Jeff to move in with me. Of course, he was in med school, so he couldn't afford much rent. I told him not to worry about it. I'd cover it. And then the tuition was due. But he was so sweet and said we were both working toward a better future. What was I going to do? I was making good money and he couldn't even pay his tuition. I put that bastard through med school. Then he got a residency in Atlanta. Atlanta! When I told him I didn't want to live in Atlanta he said it was just as well. He told me we'd grown apart and he was going alone."

He heard her bitterness. Seemed he wasn't the only one who'd been dumped. Now she jabbed him with her elbow, and he understood she was overcome with fury or sadness, too much so to talk. The fiery painful conversation ball was back in his lap.

"I believed Sarah when she said she had to work late all the time and that travel was part of the job. I was working crazy hours, too, getting my business off the ground and I figured after we got married things would calm down. Two weeks before our wedding she admitted she was having an affair with her boss." He shook his head in disgust. "The idea of her marrying someone else made him so crazy, he agreed to get a divorce. He's got three kids, by the way."

"And, I'm guessing, a lot of money?"

"She was a finance major."

"Bitch."

"Yeah."

"So, did you get even?"

If getting even involved getting drunk every night for a week, and even at his darkest, crying over her picture, then yeah, he'd gotten even all right. "No. I acted noble. Pretended I didn't care. I left my parents to deal with her parents and cancel everything and I came up here."

"Know what I did?"

"No."

A smile curled on her face. "First, I glued the pages together of every medical book he owned. And I crossed his name off his medical school diploma and wrote mine in felt pen. I figured I paid for that degree, it was at least half-mine."

"Good one." He laughed, suddenly, seeing for the first time the comical side of his own breakup. "Did it help?"

"Not really. But it was only money. What the hell? And I learned a good lesson. I'll never let any man use me again."

"I did one thing. I guess I didn't see it as revenge at the time, but I was so messed up I didn't know what I was doing for the first couple of weeks. I passed a dog shelter one day and went in. Next thing I knew, I was walking out with Buddy. The look on her face when we came through the door. I said I was exchanging one bitch for another."

Rita laughed hard and full. It was one thing he loved about her, her laugh. "And Buddy's a male dog."

"Yeah." He found himself laughing for the first time about the breakup. Nothing about it had seemed humorous until this moment. "Don't think Sarah knew that, though."

Rita suddenly sobered, and rested her head against his shoulder. "And you keep punishing women."

She was back to that again? Irritation spurted in his gut, hot and burning. "I don't punish women."

She kissed him. "I gotta go."

12

Beachcomber

1 oz light rum
1/2 oz triple sec
1/2 oz lime juice
Dash of maraschino liqueur
Sugar

Dress the rim of a cocktail glass with lime juice
and granulated sugar. Shake triple sec, lime juice,
rum and maraschino liqueur in a cocktail shaker
with cracked ice. Strain into sugared glass.

JOHNNY WOKE with the sense that something was different. Took him a minute to fully realize that he was
alone in bed and there were stealthy noises indicating
that his companion of the evening was dressing.

He yawned so wide his jaw cracked. "Morning."

She was almost finished dressing, so he'd missed the
best part. She started guiltily at his greeting. "I'm so
sorry. I was trying not to wake you."

"What time is it?"

"Eight. Go back to sleep."

He felt as if there were sandbags on top of his

eyelids. They hadn't been asleep for long. "What are you doing up? Come back to bed."

"I have to work." She sounded awfully perky for someone who couldn't have had more than three hours of sleep.

"This 'me working at night and you working in the day' thing is going to be a problem." He yawned again. "What time do you finish?"

"Today? Maybe around six."

"Come in and have dinner, then I have to start creating a martini. You can help."

"Me? I don't know how to mix a martini."

"Every martini needs a muse. Didn't you know that?"

"No. I didn't." She flashed him a delighted smile. "I've never been a muse before. Sure, I'll come by later."

"Good." He yawned again. "Hey, you don't suddenly have loyalty to the Hennington do you? Since you're consulting there?"

"Of course I have loyalty. It's something I give all my clients." She sounded a little snippy, as though he might accuse her of stealing the little soaps and shampoos or something.

"But not so much loyalty you'd be a corporate cocktail spy?"

She laughed, as if it was a funny, funny joke. "No. I promise on my honor not to reveal your secrets to Rita. Or vice versa. Not that I know any of Rita's secrets."

"Good. I'll see if I can get somebody else to close for me, then I can leave early."

She didn't look as thrilled as he'd imagined she

would after the night they'd spent together. In fact, there was a crease between her brows. "Should you be cutting short your hours? I mean, you've got the rent to pay and you don't even have a roommate sharing costs. I don't want to put you in a position where—"

"Natalie, it's fine. I won't get thrown out to make my living beachcombing. Trust me."

He could tell her that he owned the place free and clear, plus some other real estate, but he was used to letting people think whatever they liked about him, and judging him or not as they saw fit. He couldn't be bothered to explain—especially to a management consultant he'd just had sex with—that on paper at least, he was a very well-off guy.

Not at eight o'clock in the morning. He sure as hell didn't want any free advice on how he could get more rent out of his tenants or improve efficiencies or whatever she told people to do.

He was happy. Everything in his life worked.

End of story.

He scrubbed his hands over his face. "Take my bike."

"It's okay. I found the number of that cab company and called them. They should be here any minute."

She walked over to the bed, sat beside him. He wrapped his arms around her waist. "Wish you didn't have to go. We barely got started last night."

"I know." She went a little pink around the cheeks and he had a feeling she was reminiscing about their night together. "I'm looking forward to tonight."

She kissed him, then before he could drag her back down beside him, she jumped up and grabbed her straw bag. "See you later."

And she was gone.

The weather continued warmer than usual and he found himself out back, repairing a couple of loose sections on his deck when Ben came stomping around the outside of the house and found him.

"How did you know she wasn't still here?"

"I heard you hammering nails. Figured it was the masochistic activity of a guy who didn't get nailed last night."

"Very funny."

"She's cute."

"Yeah. Nice woman."

Ben paced, restless and moody. When he knelt to inspect Johnny's work and criticized his choice of wood, the gauge of nails and the way he was tackling the job, Johnny shoved the hammer at him. "You do it. I'll make some coffee."

"I'll get the proper stuff from my truck. You should have asked me for help."

He didn't think he needed it for a simple repair, but he thought Ben did need to hit stuff and make noise, so he made a noncommittal grunt and made his way into the kitchen.

He had to admit, when he returned, that Ben was doing a better job. He also seemed to really want to hammer something. "What's up with you?" he asked after the two of them had finished the job.

"Nothing."

They'd known each other for years and he wasn't fooled. "Woman trouble?"

"Maybe."

"I didn't think you were seeing anyone. You left the party alone last night. And you didn't need to."

Ben threw the hammer down, so it bounced and clattered to the wooden surface. The gesture was so unlike him, he who treated his tools with more respect than a lot of people show their kids, that Johnny knew something was seriously wrong.

"I'm being used for sex."

Johnny sat back on his heels and let the grin out. "You ho."

"Yeah, laugh. Must seem pretty funny, but it's not."

"Who is she?"

His old friend looked almost murderous. "I'm not allowed to tell. She says anyone finds out and it's over."

"Oh, man. Don't you know to stay away from married women?"

Ben spoke through gritted teeth. "She's not married. She thinks I punish women. That's what she said to me."

"When?"

"Last night."

"You seemed okay when you dropped us off."

"She told me later. She dropped by at four in the morning." He snorted. "And that's another thing. This whole relationship is based on when she feels like dropping by my place."

"How often does she drop by?"

Ben glowered at him. "Every damn night."

"For how long?"

"Five, six weeks."

"That's like a long term relationship for you since…"

"Don't you say it. Don't start. I am not punishing women because of Sarah. I wised up, that's all."

"So this mystery chick should be perfect for you.

She comes by, nails you and doesn't want anything. What are you so ticked off about?"

"What if I want more?" He roared the words.

Johnny started to think that the long, bleak winter that had been Ben's personal life since Sarah dumped him might finally be starting to thaw.

He sure hoped this woman banging him didn't mess him up more than he'd already been messed up. If she was smart enough to figure out he was punishing women, maybe she was also smart enough to help him recover. He wished he knew who she was.

"She hot?"

His answer was a cross between a snort of laughter and a heartfelt groan. "Oh, yeah, she's hot."

"You want to show her off? Make sure everybody knows what a stud you are?" Johnny watched him carefully.

"Oh, yeah. That's what I like to do. Shit, you're as bad as she is. Do you think I'm that worthless?"

"I'm trying to figure out what you want. She sounds to me like your ideal woman."

"I want to have dinner with her and talk when we actually have our clothes on. I want to call her and see if she's free to go away for the weekend. I want—"

"You want a real relationship."

"Yeah."

"Think you can handle one?"

"Yes!"

"Then go get her."

NATALIE WALKED into the Driftwood and when she saw Johnny in his usual place behind the bar her stomach did a weird flipping thing. Excitement, the pleasure of seeing him and the kick of sexual promise all combined.

As though he felt her gaze on him, he raised his head and looked right at her. His face lit up and she knew she had the same goofy expression.

Luckily, there was no one sitting at the bar, so when she climbed onto the stool, he said, "I thought about you today."

"Me, too."

"Good. You want dinner now or are you ready to work?"

"Reporting for duty, sir."

"First taste. Tell me what you think."

He handed her a drink that was turquoise and tasted like mint and some fruit. "It's good."

"Good but not great?"

"Right."

"I know." He rubbed his hands together. "I need a theme, or a place to start. I was going for a day on the ocean, but it's not inspiring me."

"Are you choking under pressure? Because you lost last year—" she held up a finger "—and to a woman, do I detect a certain competitive zeal?"

"Damn right, you do."

"Okay. Let's do it."

"Do you have any ideas for a theme?"

"After last night, all I can think of is sex." She gasped. "Did I say that out loud?"

But from his extremely pleased-with-himself expression, it was clear she had. "All I can think about, too." He threw up his hands. "Well, it's settled then. You are my muse and this year's martini will be inspired by sex." He leaned closer. She could see where stubble was beginning to appear across his cheeks, and noticed he had light freckles on his skin.

"Well, we can't work on it here," she said, shooting a scandalized look around the dining room—half empty, but still!

"Nope. We're going on a road trip."

"I haven't had dinner yet," she complained. The smells of the restaurant were making her stomach growl.

"We'll eat on the way. It's dead in here tonight. They don't need me."

"Great."

He organized one of the waiters to cover the bar and then said, "Give me a minute to get us a ride."

"Actually, I have one."

"You do?"

"I rented a car today. Seems I'm doing more driving than I thought I would."

"Smart lady. Let's go."

He directed her to an unimposing little place that was more of a shack than an actual restaurant. She'd never dated anyone for whom money was a real issue before, so she said nothing and wondered how she could pay for dinner in a way that wasn't threatening to him or his ego.

Once inside, however, it turned out to be a funky little place with modern stained glass panels for room dividers and work by local artists on the walls. The food was divided between fresh seafood, all from sustainable sources, the chalkboard menu assured, and vegetarian and vegan dishes.

The clientele was as eclectic as the menu. Men with ponytails and earrings and sharp looking guys who probably wore suits to work. Women who looked as though they'd never been near a makeup counter except to protest animal testing, and some who looked as though they didn't even get out of bed until their makeup was flawless.

"What a great place."

"Food's fantastic."

They were just being served when Johnny's friend Ben walked in with a younger guy, both in work clothes.

Ben paused to slap Johnny on the back and say hello to Natalie on his way to his table.

After he and his workmate were seated on the other side of the room, Johnny said, "I'm worried about him. He's got woman trouble."

"Really?"

"Yeah. Some mystery woman. He won't tell me who she is, but she must be local. She won't be seen with him in public. She's treating him like her boy toy. It's driving him nuts."

"What's he going to do about his problem?"

"No idea." He inched closer. "Right now I am more interested in my problems."

She couldn't resist the light teasing in his tone. "And what are your problems?"

"How to invent a winning cocktail by Friday while at the same time getting in enough sex with a desirable woman who works different hours than I do."

"I don't like to boast, but I am extremely good at what I do. As an efficiency expert I can tell you that you need to combine tasks."

"Combine tasks? You mean mix drinks and have sex at the same time?"

"Why not?"

The table moved as he shifted in his seat. "I recommend the chef's seafood salad."

"Is that their specialty?" she asked.

"No. It's the fastest thing on the menu."

"Are you telling me, that because I just said the word *sex* you now have to go have some?"

"Oh," he groaned theatrically, "you said it again."

13

Sailor's Delight

1 1/2 oz Amaretto
1 oz Southern Comfort
1/2 oz tequila
1/2 oz vodka
1 splash grenadine
1/2 glass sour mix

AT THAT MOMENT the waitress came to take their order. "I'll have the chef salad," she said, handing the woman her menu.

"Make it two."

"Be right out."

The glance he sent her was so full of promise her toes curled inside her shoes. Her skin felt hot, as though he were already touching it. From the expression on his face, she knew he was thinking about the same things she was.

When their food came they ate fast. For sustenance. Knowing they'd need it. They barely spoke as they munched their way through greens, seafood and assorted veggies. She pictured ranch hands chowing down quickly before hoisting themselves back into the saddle.

She gulped iced tea, enjoying the tart sweetness on her tongue. Even in her haste, she was noticing all the flavors of what she was eating and drinking. It was as if her senses had sharpened, from the way her skin warmed with the promise of his touch to the way her smell and taste, even her eyesight seemed sharper.

She pulled out money and noticed him doing the same. She put a hand on his arm. "Please, I want to."

A flash of something crossed the surface of his eyes. It wasn't embarrassment or annoyance. She thought it might be amusement, though what was so funny about a woman picking up the tab in a restaurant escaped her.

"Thanks," he muttered and shoved his wallet back in his pants. She left a generous tip—she'd waitressed in college and had been left with the permanent desire to reward anyone who worked in the business—and they left, almost sprinting to the car.

"Does this thing go any faster?" he complained as she drove the speed limit toward his place. For some reason this struck her as exquisitely funny and she laughed so hard she snorted. She did not, however, increase her speed.

"Safety first," she said when she stopped laughing. "And I don't mean condoms."

"Know what I'm going to do first when we get to my place?"

She swallowed, her mouth feeling suddenly dry. "No. No, I don't."

He chuckled, kind of an evil sound. "Good. Use your imagination."

"Did you want to give me any hints?"

He touched her knee, then let his hand trace up her thigh. "Yes. You'll be naked."

"Oh, will I?"

"Yep."

"And will I like whatever it is you plan to do to me?" Her voice sounded breathy and pretty much gave away her excitement.

"Oh, yeah."

Since his fingers trailed seductively up and down her thigh the rest of the time they were in the car, she considered it a minor miracle, and a matter of some pride and self-control that they made it to his place at all.

When she got out of the car, the surf called to her, sure and steady. She was so far gone that the sound of the ocean outside the guy's house was enough to make her horny. If she kept this up much longer, she'd never be able to take a cruise without embarrassing herself.

"What are you smiling about?"

"I was thinking about cruises."

"Really?" He wrapped his warm hand around her wrist and led her around the side of the house. "What about them?"

She paused before answering until she came up with, "How romantic it would be. I've never been on a cruise, but I always thought it would be nice."

"I'll take you on a cruise."

She chuckled. "You will?"

"Sure. A short cruise. Overnight."

He was leading her down the dock, toward his sailboat.

"When?"

"Right now."

"Shouldn't we be making martinis?"

His lips touched the back of her neck, so softly she thought at first it was the brush of her own hair. Then she felt the trail of his lips, warm and sexy, leaving a trail of heat behind them. "You have too many shoulds."

And some people didn't have enough. "Shoulds help a person get things done."

"I know, like to-do lists and those infernal BlackBerry PDAs." He resumed, leading her to his boat. "Sometimes, when you don't spend so much of your life planning and organizing, you have more time to actually do stuff."

"As a certified efficiency expert, I have to—"

"Shut up," he said, but so good naturedly, she sighed and gave it up.

"Your boat doesn't look ready to sail."

"It will be." He turned to her. "Okay, if you're going to get all bent out of shape about what we should be doing—" he made those annoying finger quotes around the word *should* "—then why don't you go up to the house and get out the gin, vodka, some juices, whatever looks interesting."

"This is how you design a drink?"

"Yeah, and I won the competition a bunch of times."

"The competition is stiffer now," she reminded him.

"Go. And bring the loaf of bread you'll find on the counter and some cheese."

"What's that for, to cleanse our palates?"

"No. It's in case we get hungry."

She rolled her eyes at him, but did as he told her. She found an all-but-overflowing cupboard of liquor. Picked a bottle of vodka, two liquors based on color alone, green and a sort of purple, then went into the fridge where he had an assortment of juices. She picked up guava, mango and passion fruit. The bread was an artisan loaf and the cheese was local and organic. She added a couple of apples and a pear that she found in the fridge. She took stock of her own supplies. Since she'd planned to sleep over, she had a toothbrush and fresh underwear and her traveling makeup kit.

She hadn't planned to go sailing, but then with Johnny it didn't seem that a lot of planning ever got done.

She packed the stuff in her own straw bag and a jute shopping bag he had hanging up.

Then she headed down to the dock. By this time, Johnny had everything ready. "Let's go."

"Don't you need to lock up the house?"

"Front door's locked. It's just the back that's open. It'll be fine."

"If something happens when we're gone and the owners find out, they're going to be pissed."

He looked at her oddly. "You're right about that."

"Who does own the house, anyway?"

"A guy who pretty much lets me do whatever I want. It's a good arrangement."

"Wow. Do you think he'll ever want to move in?"

Johnny was busy pushing off, and he jumped in after her. "I think he'll probably retire there."

"Hopefully not for a while."

"Yeah, hopefully not for a long while."

He patted her behind. "Okay, sous bartender, get the stuff stowed down below."

"How will you sail and pour at the same time?"

"We're not going far. Put the stuff down below and then come on back up."

"If you say so." She had visions of Rita walking off with this year's trophy and feeling guilty because she'd distracted Johnny so badly.

But it seemed she hadn't entirely ruined him for work.

After she'd put the things in the tiny fridge and in a cupboard above, she returned.

"What did you bring?"

She told him.

"Interesting. Why did you choose that combination?"

Her nose scrunched up as she considered the question. "I think I liked the colors."

"Passion fruit and guava with vodka. Needs a kick of something else." She could imagine him combining the flavors in his mouth from memory. She was certain his tongue moved as though he were tasting. "Something to add a kick. Sake? Something unexpected."

He'd hoisted the mainsail while he talked and the breeze immediately filled the white triangle, like a huge billowing shark fin.

They were skimming across the waves already, the small boat sure and swift. The sun off the water dazzled her, even in her dark glasses.

"Take the rudder," he instructed her.

"Okay." Now that she'd done this once, she wasn't as nervous. In fact, she liked being his crew.

She'd imagined they'd be tearing off their clothes and jumping each other the second they got to his place, and she imagined they would have, had she not made that silly comment about cruising. Note to self: remember Johnny is the spontaneous type.

Now she was out on the water for a sailboat sleepover. She had no idea what it would be like sleeping on a sailboat. Those sleeping quarters looked pretty tight. What if she got claustrophobic? Or the boat rocked all night and she got seasick?

Well, she was here now. And whatever hardships

were in store, she also knew that she and Johnny would be having sex. Somehow, that fact trumped all the rest.

A warmth was stealing through her, just looking at him, so at home, so efficient and in control of his small kingdom on the water. It reminded her of his other small world, the one behind the bar.

The wind picked up and as they were dancing over the waves, a dolphin jumped. She cried out with pleasure, and pointed, only to see three or four others surface, pale gray and slick, their dorsal fins gleaming. They played in the water for a bit and then, as suddenly, on some signal she couldn't see or hear, they left.

"That was amazing," she cried.

He looked back at her and she thought he was laughing at her. "Yeah. We picked a good night to come out." He gestured to the sun, hanging low. "Your basic romantic sunset cruise."

Okay, maybe he wasn't laughing at her. Maybe he was simply having a good time. She filled her lungs with sea air. The low hills along the coastline were going smudgy.

He turned to look at her over his shoulder and grinned, reminding her suddenly of a scruffy pirate. "You said you wanted to try some new things. You ever had sex on a boat before?"

Her idea of new things had mostly involved a couple of positions she'd seen in magazines that had appealed to her, but she was willing to be flexible. "No. And I have a feeling I am about to."

They sailed south, skirting close to the coastline, and when the sun set, they stood together, watching. For an odd moment she felt a lump form in her throat and wondered if she'd ever been quite so happy.

They anchored in a tiny bay. It was obvious he knew

this coastline intimately. As darkness fell, he lit lamps and she felt as though she was in the middle of some magical nowhere. No responsibilities, no worries. No one even knew where she was. The boat rocked gently over the swells.

She sighed with deep contentment and then Johnny's arms came around her and he was kissing her. Oh, how that man could kiss.

She leaned into him, loving the feel of his body, the warmth of his skin. His hands slipped under her shirt and suddenly that frantic eagerness she'd imagined earlier was happening now.

Tiny sounds came out of her throat as she grabbed at his clothes, pulling off his T-shirt, tugging down his shorts.

"Need you, now," she panted.

His reply was a wordless grunt as he unclasped her bra and freed her aching breasts. This thing they had between them was explosive. Completely out of her range of experience and very welcome.

The breeze was an extra caress against her sensitive nipples, almost like someone blowing on them. Johnny's warm palms blocked the gentle wind and then when he moved them tiny gusts tickled her sensitive flesh again.

He kissed her lips, then moved south, replacing his hands with his mouth, hot and wet as he sucked and licked at her nipples, igniting sensation that traveled like electric currents down to her core. As his mouth left one engorged peak to travel to the other, the wet nipples were licked all over again by the cooler tongue of the breeze.

Her legs couldn't hold her up, and so she half sank,

half tumbled to the deck. It was still warm from the sun, but hard. She found her discarded sweatshirt and his shirt and shoved them beneath her, lumpy but at least soft.

Then she forgot about her back as his mouth kept on going south.

Her jeans practically tugged themselves off her legs so anxious was she to be rid of them. She raised her hips and in one smooth motion Johnny had them off her, along with her panties.

Above her, stars were beginning to glow, and when he spread her thighs and put his mouth on her, she felt as though her clit was glowing as bright as the stars in the sky. Zinging light and heat and a growing heaviness in her womb combined with the hypnotic movement of the boat cradled in the bay.

Instinctively, his tongue followed the same rhythm, or it seemed to her that it did. She wasn't a particularly fanciful woman, quite the opposite in fact, but she felt in this moment intimately connected to the sea and the sky and the stars. She wanted this moment to last, stretched out and savored, but the more she fell into the blissful present, the more she felt Johnny's pleasure in her, and her own building excitement, the more impossible it became to hold back. As she climbed to the inevitable peak, she stretched her arms wide, felt her chest rise and when the intense pleasure spilled over, she thrashed, noisily and sloppily, so that the boat made its own waves.

She smiled smugly, thinking of the ripples she'd created heading out to sea in ever-softer circles, very much like the aftershocks that were pulsing through her body.

"Stand up," he ordered her softly.

She wasn't sure she could, and she found that her legs were a bit wobbly, but they held her. He led her forward and said, "Hold on."

There wasn't much to hold on to, but a narrow rail about waist height. She felt a little like Kate Winslet on the miniature version of the *Titanic*. Only this movie was definitely heading into R territory. She was naked, still trembling, as she leaned over and gripped the rail. She heard the condom pack tear open, and then a moment later, he entered her slowly.

"How are you liking your cruise?" he whispered, his body deeply connected with hers.

"Really, really enjoying it," she managed as he started to move inside her, faster now, hands on her breasts, now on her hips, an arm around her waist supporting her as her legs went to jelly and pleasure swamped her once more.

The hills were now only darker cutouts against the navy sky. This little bay was private, cut off from civilization it seemed. Theirs alone.

A drop of sweat landed on her back as he took her, his hips bumping against her as he thrust harder. The hand that wasn't supporting her reached down in front, stroking her clit, still slick and swollen.

"No," she groaned, "I don't think I can," and then she found heat building again, fast and out of control.

She was panting, pushing back against him so his cock hit her G-spot, grinding herself against his hips, while he stroked her, stoked her until she felt him stiffen and let out a cry. It was all she needed to send her over the edge one more time.

They stayed, slumped over, breathing hard, for a

long time before he kissed the back of her neck, then eased slowly away from her.

"That was amazing," she said, half to herself.

From the deep, satisfied chuckle behind her, she had to assume he'd heard. And agreed.

Too lazy to put her bra back on—what was the point when it would come off again soon enough?—she snuggled into his hoodie, and her panties and jeans. She left her feet bare.

He threw his clothes back on and then said, "You wait right here. I'm bringing you up a drink."

"A martini?"

"Of course. This is a work night, remember?"

She grinned, then followed him down.

Below deck was…well, cozy was the only way to describe it. Bench seats that she knew made into a bed, a built-in table. Built-in everything, of course. Johnny was washing the passion fruit when she got there and muttering to himself.

The propane lighting was functional, but definitely not romantic. She spotted a lantern.

"Can I take that up on deck?"

"Hmm? Yeah, sure."

He lit it for her, and she carried the square lantern up on deck along with a big fleece throw from the bench. She had a cozy sitting area out on deck when he came up with a drink.

"Now, you can't see the exact color in this light, but it's a blue-green. I tried to mimic the color of the sea." He handed it to her. "What do you think?"

"I like it."

"I'll add a bit of seaweed or something as a garnish."

"Seaweed?"

"Too much? The trick to a winning martini is to make it the same only different. I don't want to get too far from the roots. There's people putting food and stuff into the cocktails so you think, is that a drink or a meal?"

She imagined seaweed in the drink, immediately seeing the dark Nori that wrapped sushi. "A Sushi-tini?"

He groaned. "Believe me, it's been tried."

She sipped it. "Oh, yum."

"Too girlie?"

"What sort of question is that? I like it. It's fruity, but has a kick to it. Does it have a name?"

"I don't know. Something about cruising?"

"Tom Cruise?"

"Very funny. Cruise Missile?"

"Cruise Control."

"Cruise Control." He nodded. "I like it."

He sipped from her glass. "Still too bland. Wait a minute." He took the drink and left again.

She wondered what would be coming next. She had a feeling that life with Johnny was all about wondering what came next. It was a big part of his charm, especially to a woman like her who always knew what came next. Tried to, at least.

Johnny was the most spontaneous thing she'd ever done in her life. So far it was working out. Too well, in fact. Leaving was going to be tough.

But she refused to think about that right now. Not when a gorgeous, sexy bartender was brewing up a brand-new drink, and she, his muse, reclined off the coast of Southern California.

Floating.

14

Lip Lock

1/2 oz light rum
1/2 oz coconut rum
3 drops grenadine
1/2 tsp. pineapple juice
1/2 tsp. orange juice

Serve in a shot glass.

RITA WAS IN A BAD MOOD.

Again.

And when Rita was in a bad mood, sensible people stayed away. Waiters gave their drink orders in tentative voices, always with a question mark at the end as if asking her permission. "A glass of house white and two Bellinis?" Sounding to her like "if it's not too much trouble." Fools.

Right now the biggest fool of all was making a beeline for her with a swagger, his dark eyes never leaving her face.

She knew a challenge when one marched into her space.

She came right out from behind the bar, like a goalie

roaring out to face down the opposition, before it had a chance to score in her net.

They closed in on each other. Stopped maybe a foot apart. "Thought you were working on the roof today," she said. He'd already been working, apparent from his rumpled work shirt and the slight odor of working man that emanated from him. She had to resist the urge to take that one step closer and bury her nose against his sun-warmed skin. Stupid, stupid woman. She even liked the smell of his sweat.

"I am. Came in to give you something."

"What?"

"Something you forgot at my place last night." His voice lowered and she suddenly felt flooded with the warmth of memory. The words *last night* were as good as a portal transporting her back to those hours of heat, skin against skin, mouth against mouth. His groan when he entered her, the way their bodies communicated at night in a way they were unable to do in the daytime.

He put a hand in his pocket, pulled it out; she saw a flash of silver. He picked up her hand, opened the fingers and placed a silver chandelier earring in her palm. She saw herself thrashing around on the bed, wild, mad for him. Somehow she felt that an earring wasn't all she'd lost in his bed.

Therefore her bad mood.

She stared at the earring, winking at her like a friend with a secret. She closed her fingers over it, glanced up to find an expression not unlike the one she was carrying around on Ben's face. And what did he have to be pissed about?

"Thanks. But I could have picked it up tonight."

"How do I know you're coming over tonight?"

He said it in a challenging tone. She could let it go or she could take up the challenge. Frankly, the idea of letting off a little steam was too appealing not to go for it.

"Don't you want me to come over?"

Something hot and desperate flashed across his face, then he resumed the stone faced expression he'd worn before. "Up to you."

He took a step away, started to turn, then he startled her by suddenly stamping back to her. "It's not like I have a choice. It's not like we ever plan ahead."

"What do you want from me?"

"A normal dinner out would be nice. Some notice that you're coming over to hump me."

He sounded so aggrieved, so like how women sounded when complaining about men, that she almost lost it and laughed. Except that this was too serious to laugh about.

"Maybe we should take a break, you go with one of those women who are okay doing dinner, a little hot sex and then getting forgotten." She glanced significantly to where Stephanie was setting up tables for lunch in the dining room.

He followed her gaze and when his attention returned to her he looked as if he wanted to hit something. "I don't want any other women. I want you."

"Do you?"

"I—" He looked so shocked by his own words that she pretty much had her answer. If they hadn't been in her workplace, she'd probably have hugged him, he looked so lost and angry, without even understanding why.

"You think about that." She started to retreat back behind the bar, then found her wrist gripped.

"Will I see you tonight?"

She could be flip, she could toy with him, she could refuse to play this stupid game anymore. Instead she nodded. "Yeah."

A brief up-and-down motion of his head was the only acknowledgment. He turned and left, stopping to say a brief hello to Natalie, who strolled into the restaurant looking like a completely new woman from the serious workaholic of a few days ago.

She came over and sat up at the bar. "Hey."

"You might want to take a seat in the restaurant. I'm in a pissy mood." Rita's expression was bleak.

"So I see." She set her bag down, made sure her BlackBerry was beside her on the bar.

"No cell phones in the restaurant."

"I turned off the ring tone. It will flash if I get a call. Which I will take outside."

"Suit yourself."

Natalie seemed to be the only person in Orca Bay who wasn't affected by Rita's mood. But then she hadn't been here long. Rita slapped a menu down in front of her and turned her back on the woman; she had things to do after all.

She felt herself being observed. A glance at Natalie had her feeling suddenly defensive. "What?"

"I was just thinking, I haven't interviewed you yet. I think you might have some good insights into how we could improve efficiency."

She snorted. "I'm a bartender, not management."

"Come on. It's people on the floor who see the operation at the customer level. How about we sit at a table and I buy you lunch?"

"I'm in a bad mood," she repeated.

"So you said. And I am in an exceptionally good mood. Euphoric in fact. We'll balance each other out."

"You're bossy, you know that?"

"Not everyone understands that about me right up front."

"Cause you're sneaky about it."

But she grudgingly asked Steph to watch the bar and took a table in the far corner where no one would bother them. "Is that why you're so early for lunch? So you could interview me?"

"Partly. Also, I was hungry."

Miguel, one of her favorite waiters because he minded his own business—another reason she'd sat them here—came over instantly.

"Good morning, ladies." He treated her like another customer. "Can I get you anything to drink to start?"

"Iced tea, please," said Natalie.

She nodded. "Same for me."

"I'll leave you with your menus for a minute," he said in his lilting accent. He was from Mexico City and that was almost all she knew about him. "Today's specials are Ahi tuna lightly grilled in a pecan crust, and fresh seafood salad." As if she didn't know.

The minute he was gone, Natalie asked, "How is the seafood salad?"

"Amazing. Have it."

So they did.

Once Miguel had delivered the teas and made himself invisible once more, she said, "So, what do you want to know?"

"How long have you been sleeping with Ben?"

Rita's eyes narrowed. "It's a good thing I wasn't in the middle of drinking my iced tea, or I'd have sprayed it all over you. What makes you think I'm sleeping with Ben?"

"I figured there was something up between you at the party the other night. The second he came up to us, you got tense and walked away. When he tried to approach you in the kitchen, you became Rita the manic bartender. Watching you two just now when I came in confirmed my suspicions."

"But we were arguing?"

"Your body language wasn't. You two were in each other's personal space, you leaned in to each other. I saw his face when he walked away from you, and yours watching him go."

"You're smarter than every person in Orca Bay."

"I have a very high IQ." She grinned. "I'm also an outsider. I see things the locals don't because I have no preconceived notions. It's why hiring outside consultants is such a good idea for businesses."

"I don't know how you just related those two things, but whatever."

"So?"

Rita stared at her for a moment, considering. She glanced around the room, but no one was anywhere near them. Or interested enough to eavesdrop. "You tell no one. Understand?" she said in a fierce whisper.

"You gave me some pretty good advice about Johnny. I'd like to help you out, too. Besides, I feel like we're becoming friends," she said, sounding tentative.

Rita let out a breath. "I guess I could use a friend about now." She glanced around. "You can't tell Johnny."

"I won't tell anyone. But Johnny knows something's up. I think Ben told him he's having woman issues, but he wouldn't say with who."

"Woman issues. Hah. He has 'I got dumped at the altar and now I have to punish every woman I meet' issues."

"Yeah. I heard about his history. That sucks."

"Sucks being in love with the guy, too." Then she dropped her head in her hands. "Did I just say that out loud? Oh, my God. I'm getting as bad as you. I haven't even said it to myself, quietly, in my head. I can't go there. I can't. That man will make me crazy."

"I couldn't help noticing that you make him a little crazy, too."

Rita smiled, probably for the first time all day. "I figured he'd be good for some recreation." She shrugged, thinking about how she and Ben had started. "I like sex, and we sure do burn up the sheets. But no way I am letting that man be seen with me, you know? He goes through a new woman faster than a tank of gas. And in that stupid big pig of a truck he drives, that's not a long time."

"How many tanks of gas have you two been together?"

They stopped when Miguel brought their salads, heaped with Dungeness crab, scallops and chunks of fresh halibut on mixed greens with a wonderful dressing—the chef wouldn't reveal the ingredients. She tasted ginger and sesame and the rest was a delectable mystery.

He placed a basket of fresh, warm bread on the table and left them.

"Enjoy," she said, realizing she was hungry, too. She'd barely eaten anything this morning.

Natalie stabbed a forkful of crab and greens, chewed and moaned with pleasure. "Oh, it's soo good."

"I know. Fifty bucks if you can get chef to share his dressing recipe."

Natalie grinned, her eyes were sparkling and a light tan had given her a healthy glow. Also, there was no mistaking that she looked like a woman getting some very nice sex.

She was also not one to lose the thread of an interrupted conversation. "So, how long have you two been, you know, intimate?"

"Six weeks."

"And how often do you see each other?"

"Every night."

Natalie stopped chewing and stared. "So, you're exclusive?"

"Unless he's screwing women on his lunch hours, which I doubt, then yeah, we're exclusive."

"And you're together every single night."

She shifted uncomfortably. "Yeah. I go over to his place. We have a deal where if he's parked his truck under cover, he's otherwise engaged, but every night when I drive by, there it is, empty and waiting for me."

"So you have nights of complete intimacy and in the day you act like strangers?"

"I never stay the whole night. I don't want him thinking I care or he'll freak."

"What if he cares?" Natalie had a very intense way of staring at a person when she was concentrating. "You know he cares, right?"

She'd told Natalie more than she'd told anyone. She might as well be completely honest. "Yeah. I know." She dropped her gaze to the tabletop. "But how much does he care? That's the question. I've been a fool to fall for him. I never meant to."

"I know how that is."

She glanced up sharply. "You, too?"

"Well, I'm not in love with Johnny." She gulped visibly. "You can't fall in love in a few days, right? But he's fun and he makes me laugh and—"

"You're having the best sex of your life."

Natalie's blush gave her away. "Yeah, and then there's that." She took a sip of her drink, put down the glass and waved her hand as though batting the idea of her being in love far away. "Still my relationship is governed by a ticking clock. Yours isn't. So, what are you going to do about Ben?"

Looking outside the dining room window reminded Rita how beautiful this place was. How much she loved it. She didn't want to screw this thing up so badly she'd feel she needed to move on. "You're the management consultant. You tell me how to manage this mess."

"Okay, here's how I see it. You are together every night. He's getting angry that you won't see him in the day. What would you do if he asked you out on a date?"

She winced. "He did. He does. A lot. It's really pissing him off that I won't go."

"Then you need to decide how much you are willing to invest, how much you're willing to risk."

"That's management speak for?"

"For what are you prepared to do? It seems like the status quo isn't working anymore. You're in love and he's possibly in love, too, but you're both too damned scared to admit the truth to each other."

"I'm not scared."

Natalie gave her a look that said she did not believe that. "Let's substitute the word *stubborn*. Would you agree your behavior might be termed stubborn?"

"Let's say *cautious*."

The smile that came across the table was a little judgmental in Rita's opinion, but Natalie only said, "Okay, *cautious*. Now, as a cautious woman you need to decide whether being cautious but safe is more important to you than taking a big risk and possibly finding love."

"You mean, telling Ben how I feel?"

"I think you could start with going out for dinner or a movie or something in public. Letting people see you together."

She touched a hand to her breastbone. "Make myself vulnerable?"

Her friend nodded.

"I've got scars, too, you know?"

"Yeah, I know." It was said softly, but somehow she thought Natalie did understand.

Grabbing a piece of bread, she buttered it savagely. She didn't even want bread, she wanted something to do while she thought about Natalie's proposition.

"What if I leave things the way they are?"

"Sure, you could, but I get the feeling that's not really working for you anymore. Rita, you love the guy. Isn't he worth fighting for?"

"But how can I fight some little princess who dumped him and stepped all over his heart?"

Natalie straightened up and gave her a look she bet solved many a dispute. "Are you kidding me? Look who she's dealing with." And Natalie pointed right at her.

"Damn it, you're right. And if he tries to dump me, I'll kick his ass."

"And I'll stand in line behind you to kick his ass."

"Okay. I'll do it. My reputation will survive if he is too stupid to get what a good thing we have going."

"Right."

"Excellent."

"How about now?"

15

Erotic Fantasy

1 oz. Amaretto
2 oz Irish cream liqueur
1/2 oz white crème de caçao
1 oz coffee liqueur
Mango
Strawberries
Ice (crushed)

Serve over crushed ice in highball glass, garnish with mango and strawberries.

"DON'T PUSH ME."

"Somebody's got to push you or you'll mess this up. Look, you helped me get over myself and have a no-strings-attached affair with Johnny—something I never thought I'd do—and it worked out pretty well. I'm returning the favor."

Rita wasn't fooled for a second. "You ever going to forgive me for telling you what to do?"

"You mean bullying me? Yeah, I'll forgive you. When you pick up that cell phone and call Ben."

"I don't think I have his number."

"No problem. I'm sure I can get it for you."

"Okay, I have it." Rita scowled, but her horrendous mood was dissipating. She took her cell phone out of her pocket.

She'd never asked for his number and he'd never offered, but one day last week she'd turned on her phone and discovered he'd programmed his number into her phone, something he must have done while she was sleeping. The idea filled her with an odd sense of possibility.

She glanced significantly at Natalie, but she didn't move. "Do you mind? This is a private conversation."

"All I want is to know you made contact, then I'm out of here."

"You know, at moments you are scarily like me."

She chuckled. "Yeah, I know. And I have to tell you it's a lot more fun being the mentor."

Before she could lose her nerve, Rita hit Ben's number. She heard it ring, wondered what she'd do if she got a message, knew she'd hang up, and maybe that was a sign. Then he answered.

"Yeah."

The sound of his voice barking that one word made her melt in extremely inappropriate places considering she was at work. For a mortifying moment she was tongue tied, couldn't think of a single thing to say.

"Yeah!" he said again.

She pulled herself together. "I discovered this number mysteriously programmed into my phone and I figured I'd better call it."

A beat's silence followed and she pictured him as tongue tied as she had been. "You should report that. It's probably a violation of your contract with your phone company." The lazy sexiness of his voice went through her and she found herself smiling, settling back into the seat just as Natalie gave her a thumbs-up and slid from the table.

"Thought I'd call in case it was some hot guy who put his number in my phone."

"What do you think, do I sound hot?"

"Yeah, actually, you do. What do you look like?"

"You like tall blond guys?"

She pictured him there up on the roof, probably surrounded by roofing guys who could hear every word, and was filled with an urge to climb up there after him and kiss him senseless. "How did you guess, that's my favorite type of man."

"Oh, well, I don't look anything like that."

"Too bad."

"What's your second favorite type?"

She took a breath. This was it. "The type who doesn't leave the second things get tough."

"Shit," he muttered. "You don't pull punches, do you?"

"I figure my life is too short to screw around. But you sound like a pretty nice guy. I have a proposition for you."

"Yes."

Her laughter bubbled out of her, surprising even the unflappable Miguel into staring at her. "You haven't heard what the proposition is yet."

"Whatever it is, I'm in."

"I'm inviting you to go out for dinner with me tonight."

"Let me get this straight, you did say out, right?"

"Right."

"Out as in public, while it's still light out and strangers could possibly see us together?"

"Friends and acquaintances might even see us together."

"You sure about this?"

"No. I am trusting you, Ben, which is not an easy thing for me to do."

"I get it."

"So, are you free tonight?"

"No. I've got a client meeting."

"Oh." She felt stupid suddenly and wished Natalie was still here so she could kick her under the table for this horrible idea.

"Which I will reschedule so I can go out with you tonight."

"Oh, great. Okay."

"Where do you want to go?"

"I don't know."

"I've got an idea. I'll make a reservation," Ben said.

"Where are you thinking?"

He waited a beat. "Johnny's place."

"The Driftwood?" She all but shrieked the word. "All our friends either work there or hang out there. The news will be around town before midnight."

"Yep."

"But—"

"This was your idea, Rita."

"But—"

"Have you ever thought that we are together for a reason?"

"Multiple orgasms are good for me."

"Coward."

"You come down off that roof and say that again to me, to my face!"

The phone disconnected in her ear.

"Ben? Ben!"

She leaped out of her seat. Shit. She was about to bolt into the kitchen and hide when she stopped herself and, with a shake of her hair, positioned herself behind the bar with her snootiest expression on her face.

She heard some scrambling overhead, that made her smile, and then a few minutes went by before Ben charged into the dining room, thankfully deserted but for staff, with an expression on his face that made her feel as if she weighed about a hundred pounds and was about to be tossed over his shoulder and hauled off to his cave.

The idea, she had to admit in the far reaches of her prefeminist brain, had some merit.

He stalked toward her; her heart speeded up. Luckily, the bar was between them.

He stopped, narrowed his eyes, rounded the bar.

"Patrons aren't allowed behind the bar, sir."

"I'm not a patron." He came right into her space, her bar. He grabbed her, and yanking her forward, kissed her hard. He tasted like sweat and sawdust and sex.

She kissed him back.

He backed away, nodded. "I'll pick you up at eight."

"I'll be at my place."

"Fine."

"Do you know where it is?"

"I'll find it."

She licked her lips. "I have one question?"

"What?"

"What if we have nothing in common, not a single thing to talk about?"

His chest rumbled. "Don't you worry about that. I've got some things I want to say to you."

He marched out and she turned, slightly dazed to see Miguel, Stephanie and two busboys staring at her with equally stunned expressions.

"Get back to work," she snapped.

NATALIE WAS ENORMOUSLY pleased with herself as she made her way back upstairs to the admin offices. In fact, her success with Rita prompted her to organize a meeting with the front desk manager and the reservations manager, whose feud was getting in the way of smooth operations. Sometimes, people needed a little push in the right direction in order to open channels of clear communication. By five, she'd powered through her day's work and managed to maneuver two reluctant managers into agreeing to work with her to make their system smoother.

Today was a good day. Though, at the bottom of her satisfaction there lurked a tiny doubt that she'd done the right thing. What if she'd bullied Rita into going public with her relationship with Ben and something bad came of it? Of course, that was always the risk of taking an interest in someone else's affairs. You could try to solve a problem and make things worse.

So, she worried.

Her cell rang around four. "Natalie Fanshaw."

"It's Rita." The panicked tone had Natalie's heart plummeting to her emotional basement.

"What is it?"

"That man is going to make me crazy, I swear."

"It sounded like things were going pretty well on the phone when I left."

A bitter laugh met her ears. "Oh, it was going fine all right, so fine he tells me he'll make a reservation for us for dinner. Tonight."

"Okay, that's good, right?"

"Do you know where he wants to go?"

She flipped through the slim mental catalog she had of the local area. "I really don't know this part of the coast very well. Where?"

"It's a place you know well. I know well. Every person in Orca Bay knows it well."

A burble of laughter almost escaped. "You don't mean—"

"I do. The bastard's taking me to the Driftwood."

"Oh, honey, he really is having some fun with you, isn't he?"

"I was okay. I was fine. I figured 'what the hell.' It's dinner with a friend. Maybe somebody we know will see us, maybe not. We'd ease into this thing slowly. Then he throws the Driftwood at me. The news we're an item will be all over town before we order appetizers."

Natalie doubted they'd be seated before the juicy rumor was being texted from phone to phone, but she kept her opinion to herself. "You know, there's a huge upside to this, too, right?"

"I don't know anything," she snapped. Then a sound of frustration, half groan, half sigh came through the phone. "I am a strong woman. Men don't make me beg, and they don't make me cling. I don't need anyone."

"Yes, of course. I know that. Everyone knows that."

"But—I want to ask you something."

"Sure. Anything."

"I need you to be there."

This time the laughter escaped before she could contain it. "Me? You don't think a third person at dinner might cramp your date?"

"Not at the table. Just be there. Hang out with Johnny at the bar or something."

"Why?"

"I'm so freaked out, I might need some moral support. His best friend is tending bar. That makes the Driftwood too much Ben's turf. I should have my person there, too. I pick you. It's only fair, you got me into this."

"Rita, I'd be honored to be your person inside the Driftwood." Not to mention, she'd have a ringside seat on the most unlikely romance in California, excluding L.A. and Hollywood. "What time's your reservation?"

"Seven."

"I'll be there."

In the interest of not appearing too blatant, she showed up at twenty minutes before seven. The hostess was so used to her visits now she didn't even offer a table, simply waving her down toward the bar, with a quick, "Hey, Natalie!"

When she headed to the bar, and Johnny's gaze connected with hers, she experienced the breathlessness that was becoming a habit every time she saw him.

His grin dawned slowly and she was almost positive as he watched her walk toward him that he was picturing her naked. All her erogenous zones sprang to life and by the time she got close enough to slide onto a stool, all she wanted to do was grab her new lover and take him home. They had so little time together, and there was so much she wanted to experience.

His eyes drifted to her mouth and even though they didn't touch, she felt as though she were being kissed. She licked her lips.

"What can I get you?"

She whispered, "A Screaming Orgasm, and I don't mean the drink."

"You didn't get your fill last night?"

"I don't think I could ever get my fill."

For a second their gazes locked and she knew they were both thinking the same thing. How short their time together was.

He broke the moment by saying, "Order whatever you want. Your tab's taken care of."

"Johnny, you can't do that."

"I didn't. Rita called ahead. She's covering your tab."

She grinned in complete delight. "She told you?"

"Ben told me. He called me right after she called him. He said to make sure and get him and Rita the most visible table in the room."

She leaned in, feeling the intimacy between them that was becoming more than only physical. "What do you think about Ben and Rita?"

"I was blown away. I never would have guessed it was Rita. They're so—"

"Alike?"

Startled, his head jerked backward, as if her observation was a slap. "I was going to say opposite. You think they're alike?"

"Yes. They are both stubborn and scared. Pig-headed. Independent to a fault. But maybe, just maybe, smart enough not to throw away the very thing that could be the making of them both." Natalie glanced around the restaurant, hoping very much she was right.

"If she hurts him, I don't know if he'll recover a second time."

"Maybe she's the person who can heal him."

His brow creased. "Yeah. Maybe."

It was a fairly busy night at the restaurant, but fortunately no one except Natalie was at the bar.

At length she chose a glass of white wine and he didn't try to stop her. Maybe they were both too focused on the upcoming date to concentrate on fancy drinks.

However it seemed she was wrong. After she'd taken a sip of wine, he said softly, "I was thinking that I want to build a drink around a fantasy."

When his voice dropped, low and sexy like that, her belly grew heavy with arousal. She could feel the tingle zing from her nipples to her clit, hitting random hot spots in between like a pinball of lust.

"What kind of fantasy?" Her own tone sounded husky in her ears.

"Sexual. A secret, sexual fantasy."

"What have you come up with?"

"I'm asking you. I want to create an essentially female fantasy." He ran a finger down her forearm and across her knuckles, sketching out a J of sensation. "I want to create your fantasy."

She crossed her legs, shifted, crossed them the other way.

Her lips felt so dry she took another sip of wine. "You're asking me to describe a sexual fantasy so you can make a drink around it?"

"Yes."

He reached out again, seeming to lay his hand casually on the granite surface, but in fact trailing along the edge of her hand with his fingertips. Up her inner arm, almost but not quite brushing her breast. Her response was immediate and visceral. "Remember our first time together? You said there were some things you'd always wanted to try. I've been thinking about that a lot lately. I want to make one come true for you. Something you'll always remember."

"What are you going to call this drink, Natalie's Fantasy?"

"Depends on the fantasy."

The temperature seemed to be rising in the restaurant. She felt that she was wearing too many clothes, she wanted to peel them off and run naked into the ocean. Then she imagined Johnny running into the surf with her and realized she was creating a fantasy right now. "I'm really not that wild."

"I've been naked in bed with you. I know better."

A tiny smile tilted the corners of her mouth. "You think I'm wild?"

He nodded slowly. "I saw it the first time we met, remember?"

"Vintage champagne. Of course I remember." She grinned. "I think you popped my cork."

"No matter how many times I pop your cork, there's always another level I want to reach with you." The seriousness of his tone surprised her. What surprised her even more was how the words zinged through her, making her want more.

"So now you want my fantasies?"

"Only one. For my drink."

She dropped her gaze, traced the stem of her glass against the cool marble.

He didn't say a word, only waited, the air between them charged.

"My fantasy."

16

Insanitini

1 part hazelnut liquor
1 part banana liquor

Serve in a plastic glass so you don't hurt yourself.

NATALIE THOUGHT ABOUT these days she'd spent with Johnny, the passionate nights, the carefree way he made her feel. Making love on the sailboat, on a spontaneous trip, something she wouldn't have believed she'd ever partake of.

"The truth is, this is my fantasy." He looked at her quizzically and she tried to explain. "I'm always the one in control. I plan, I organize, I fix. I am so competent I scare myself. Companies love me. They nearly always offer me a job when I come in to consult. I'm very good at what I do, but some times I feel like I could use a vacation from always being so damned efficient, you know?"

"I can see how that could happen," he agreed, his eyes crinkling at the corners in that mouthwatering way.

"Then I date men who work at similar jobs and

organize their lives the way I do. Driven men who are basically the male equivalent of me." She flicked a glance up at him. "I've never indulged in a fling before. Never."

"So you're saying, this is your fantasy? It's not very exciting."

"It is for me. With you, none of that other stuff matters. I can set away all my shoulds and my obligations." She sighed at the sense of relaxation being with him gave her. "With you I can lose control."

He was listening so intently she knew he heard not only her words but probably the unspoken things she couldn't articulate. Frederick would probably think she was slumming, slaking a purely sexual hunger with someone far outside her world. She'd witnessed his contempt for colleagues who slept with flight attendants or waitresses when they were on the road—single men who had no romantic entanglements—as though they were violating some unwritten professional standard.

Perhaps, in some way, she'd internalized the same hideous snobbishness without even realizing it. So Johnny, for her, was the ultimate in forbidden fantasies. "You're not a colleague or anyone who is part of my life. You're my fling on the road. And it means I can completely lose myself with you."

"Losing control sounds like it pushes a lot of your buttons."

"Yes, I suppose so." She pushed a strand of loose hair behind her ear. "Not that I would ever want to, you know, physically lose control." She felt she should clarify based on the way he was staring at her as though plotting something extremely far from her experience or comfort zone.

"You physically lose control every time you come. It's one of my favorite things about you, the way your body takes over from your too-active mind, the way you thrash and moan—and sometimes you scr—"

"I know what I do. Shh."

His talk was reminding her that she would like to experience that very thing, and soon. Her body began to hum.

"I'm just saying, when you slip your leash, you're something else."

"Exactly." She felt the relief flow through her. "You understood what I was trying to say."

"Sure." He moved nearer. She could smell his soap and the faint scent of ocean that was part of him. Loved the way his never-ironed cotton shirt shifted across his chest. His low, husky voice was like one of his strongest cocktails, potent and seductive. "You were comparing losing control to say, being tied up."

"Hnnn" or a sound approximately like that came out of her mouth.

He'd barely moved, yet he was touching her, so she could feel the graze of his stubble on her sensitive flesh, the warmth of his breath against her hair as he dropped his voice to a whisper.

"Bondage can be a real turn-on. Especially for control freaks."

"I wouldn't know. It's certainly not something I'd be interested in trying."

"That's funny, your voice has that note it gets when you're horny, I think I saw your pulse jump, the one right here in your neck—" he touched her with his fingertip and she was sure the damned thing jumped again "—and I smell your arousal."

"It's the hotel shampoo."

He chuckled, an evil sound. "Too bad you're not into it. I'm getting some good ideas already."

"For your drink? Are you thinking of twine around the glass stem and tiny handcuffs as garnish?"

His teeth gleamed. "Not bad. But I was thinking about how I would definitely want your legs nice and wide apart when I tied you up."

She swallowed and barely resisted choking. A fan would be nice about now, a nice cool fan blowing a frosty breeze on her overheated face. They should really get the heating and cooling system at the Driftwood thoroughly checked out. "I really don't—"

"A lot of people think bondage is a simple game. Get some cuffs from the sex store, or a few silk scarves and you're in business. But they are missing the subtleties of the project."

She swallowed again. She shouldn't encourage him, but she couldn't help herself. "Subtleties?"

"Sure. I would want you helpless, bound and completely at my pleasure, but also able to move in all those ways of yours that I love."

"What ways?" She could not believe she was continuing this conversation, it was as if her inner slut had taken over her mouth.

"The way your hips do a kind of dance, sort of a figure eight, I guess would be the closest, when you get close to climaxing. I'd want to give you plenty of freedom to thrash."

"Thrash."

"And writhe."

He barely kept his grin in check.

"You're doing this deliberately."

"It's turning you on so much I think you're close to coming right now."

"You don't know that for sure." She tried to sound snooty, but she was pretty sure she sounded like a woman so turned on she was close to climax.

"I'd come around there and check, but if I walk out from behind this counter I'll embarrass myself."

She knew without checking that her nipples were straining against her shirt. "You, too?"

"Oh, yeah."

Some of the balance of power shifted when he said that, giving her more confidence. "Well, that's a problem."

"It is. I think we should do something about this problem. We should definitely try out this bondage fantasy of yours."

Her breath huffed in and out. "I don't have a bondage fantasy."

"If you didn't before, you do now." He let his gaze drop suggestively to her chest and the visible proof of her condition.

"You mean tonight?"

"No. I don't mean tonight, so don't get out your little electronic planner and pencil me in. That's part of the deal, see. You don't get to say when or where or how. You don't get to manage the project, improve its efficiency or make it happen faster. You don't even get a say."

"Of course I do—"

"No. You don't."

"But that's—"

"Going to happen. And soon."

"I can't—"

"You don't have to. You don't have to do anything."
He leaned closer to her once more. "I think I should
tell you something else."

"What?"

"I will probably blindfold you."

She was horrified by the heat crawling over her skin
as well as feeling ever so slightly panicked.

"I'd be blind?"

"Only temporarily. You'd be amazed at how your
other senses intensify when you can't see what's going
on."

"But we make love in the dark all the time."

"Not the same. You can always snap on a light.
When you have a blindfold over your eyes it's a very
different sensation. Trust me."

"I guess I'd have to, wouldn't I? I'd have to really,
really trust you."

"Do you?"

She looked up at him. What he was really asking was
simple. Did she trust him enough? Enough to give up
control? Even temporarily she knew it would be tough
for her. But something about the heat coursing through
her body suggested that on some level she really wanted
to try.

"Yes. I trust you."

He looked more than pleased, she thought. Relieved,
maybe, as though a negative response would have hurt
his feelings. Which was ridiculous. She was so on edge
she was reading things into his words.

When he glanced past her and nodded his head in
recognition, she was pretty sure she knew who had
entered the dining room. Thank goodness, this very inappropriate discussion could be interrupted. But what

kind of friend had she been to forget all about poor Rita all this time? "Ben and Rita?"

"Yep."

"How do they look?"

"Tense."

"Tense? That can't be good."

She sipped her wine and casually, oh, so casually, turned her head to observe the dining room. She saw them being led to the center table, the most visible table in the dining room. She'd never seen them together as anything but antagonists so it was interesting to watch them together and trying to be a couple. Rita had out-Rita'd herself in the wardrobe department. She wore a tight black dress that made even Natalie, who'd never had a lesbian fantasy in her life, drool. With it she wore crimson high, high heels. Her makeup was bold, her hair loose and free.

Ben looked dressed up for the occasion, as well. His shirt was white and gleamed with newness, he wore dress pants and shiny black shoes. There was a tiny hiccup in the action and noise of the room as everyone, from the waitstaff to the diners, took in the couple being seated at the center table.

She knew that Rita would know she'd been set up for the most visible table, and figure out that Ben had asked for it particularly.

And something hit her with blinding clarity.

For Rita, coming out in public with Ben was a similar test to Johnny asking Natalie if she would let him tie her up.

It was all about trust. And risk.

Rita didn't look as though she'd completely made up her mind on the trust issue.

But then, it went both ways. It was easy for Ben to believe that everything would be fine, but what if, now that they were an openly acknowledged couple, he freaked out? He was pushing that woman hard. He'd better be ready to move out of town if he let Rita down. And Natalie would personally book the moving van.

Except that she probably wouldn't be here.

Sadness stabbed at her. In such a short time she'd come to care about these people. Soon she'd be leaving, and would likely never know how it all turned out.

If trust was enough.

She turned back to Johnny. "By the way, that trust thing?"

"What about it?" He was staring at the center table as if it were the final minutes of the Super Bowl.

"Trust goes both ways, right?"

Still, he didn't look at her. "Absolutely."

"So, if I let you tie me up…"

Now she had his complete attention. His gaze locked on hers. "Uh-huh?"

She swallowed, even saying the words was hard, "And blindfold me…"

"Right."

"Then you have to let me return the favor."

He raised his eyebrows slightly, which she took to mean, go on.

"I would tie you up and blindfold you, and do whatever I wanted to you."

"But—"

"That's the deal, big boy. Take it or leave it."

He laughed low in his throat. "I'm taking it."

"Good." She glanced over at Rita and Ben, now seated. It seemed that once Rita had realized Ben had all but put them in a public spotlight, she had decided to make the most of it. She sat tall, her long legs crossed and angled to the side so she drew the eye. They were a gorgeous couple. American and exotic at the same time. Rita sat like the queen of all she surveyed. Ben, looking both proud and a little nervous, had his work cut out for him, she thought.

"Check that out," said one of the waitresses as she approached for a drink order. "We're placing bets on how long they last. You in?"

Johnny shook his head. "No. Wouldn't be right. He's my best friend."

"Yeah, you're right. You'd have an unfair advantage."

"What are the odds?" Natalie asked.

Both Johnny and the waitress stared at her.

"You want in?"

"No. I'm curious what their friends think of their chances."

"Well, Beth over there put five bucks on this being a one-night stand." She moved closer. "Course, for Beth he was a one-night stand, so she's got experience. And the longest guess is for a month, but that's Hernandez and he's new here."

17

G-Spot

1 oz Southern Comfort
1 oz raspberry liqueur
1 oz orange juice

Shake over ice, then strain into shot glasses.

"WHAT DO YOU THINK the odds are on us?" Rita asked Ben.

"Hmm?" He looked up from his menu.

"They've got a pool going on how long we'll last."

"No, they've all got better things to do."

"I've worked in a lot of restaurants. Believe me, they don't."

He leaned back a little. "Is that a problem for you?"

This whole thing was a problem for her as he knew very well, but having made up her mind, she wasn't going to let a little gossip ruin her evening.

"No. I simply need to break the pool. It's a point of pride."

In fact, now that she'd taken his dare and come out with him on an actual, old-fashioned—he picked her up at her place and walked her to his truck—date, she was enjoying herself.

She liked how Ben looked dressed up in a white, crisp shirt that she suspected was new. He'd not only taken trouble with his appearance, she thought he'd cleaned his truck. She even liked the way he read a menu with deliberation as though it were a newspaper and there was an election coming up and he hadn't yet decided who he was voting for.

She ordered a martini before dinner, curious to see how good Johnny's was. In her opinion you could tell a lot about a bartender from his or her martini. This one, she had to admit, was close to perfect. Only hers were better.

Natalie was perched at the bar, and glancing over from time to time as though ready to run over and make small talk if the date was a clear disaster. She couldn't believe she'd been such a wimp as to ask Natalie to come tonight, any more than Rita could believe she had said yes.

Too bad Natalie was leaving Orca Bay so soon. She felt she'd found a new friend. Not somebody she'd have chosen, but someone who happened into her life, which was what made their liking each other kind of crazy.

A little like love.

Which brought her attention back to her date.

"Any thoughts yet on what you're having for dinner?"

He glanced up. Noticed her closed menu. "You in a rush?"

"Not at all. I'm enjoying my martini."

He reached for her glass, helped himself to a sip, putting his lips on the spot where her lipstick had made a mark. He looked up at her over the rim as he sipped and she felt the impact as though she'd swallowed the liquor.

"It's good," he said.

She curved her lips. "Not as good as mine. We'll do a taste test, later."

"If there's time."

Their waitress wandered up. Rita wanted to ask her about the bets she was certain were being taken, but it wouldn't be fair, seeing as she was a guest here tonight, so she kept her mouth shut.

"Any questions about the menu?"

"Yes," Ben said. "Where was the tuna caught? And what kind of oil is it seared in? I also have a question about the oysters."

Wow. Cool gourmet dinner questions. Who knew? She waited until the waitress had patiently answered all his questions and left him still reading.

"I had no idea you were a fussy eater."

"I like to know where my food comes from and how it's cooked."

"It's an endearing little quirk. Or at least I think it is. I didn't know that."

"There's a lot you don't know about me."

"There are a few things you don't know about me, too."

He sipped his own drink, a beer, and raised his brows. "Tell me one."

It felt sort of strange talking to him as if they didn't know each other, when they knew each other so intimately on a physical level. She tried to think of something light and easy. "I feed Buddy. Every night I bring him treats from the restaurant. That's why he loves me so passionately."

He sat back, looking very sexy and at ease. "I know that. I didn't think he was going out for fine dining after I was in bed and bringing home doggie bags. I find them in the trash."

"Oh."

"And you can do better than that. This is a get-to-know-you dinner. A first date."

She leaned forward. "I already know all the places on your body where my tongue drives you insane."

The look he sent her told her he knew the same about her. She wondered how they'd get through this without making each other crazy. "So, the first date is a little out of order. It's still a first date. Come on. Tell me something real."

It was a relief when the waitress came. "I'll have the spinach salad to start and the seafood special."

Ben ordered the oysters and the tuna. And a bottle of wine without asking her advice. He chose pretty well, too.

"Do you even remember what the seafood special was?"

"No. But their special is always good. I trust the chef."

He shook his head. "So, you were going to tell me something?"

"I like roses."

"Roses? This is you sharing something personal? You like roses?"

But she was already far away, and the smell of summer was in her mind. "We used to have them growing all over the yard when I was a kid. My mama loved them. I used to help her out in the garden and she taught me all the names of the flowers and plants, even the herbs she grew. But, I don't ever have the time, and I've never really had a garden of my own, so I don't get the chance to grow more than a pot of geraniums on the balcony. But sometimes, if I've got some extra money, after a good night of tips, say, I buy myself a bouquet of roses. Never a dozen red, or white, I like to get them in assorted colors. They're nothing like the same as the ones that grew in our garden. But they make me feel closer to my mama."

"Do you look like your mama?"

"I think so, a little." She smiled. "How about you? Tell me something about you that I don't know."

"Let's see. I came here thinking the world had ended and I'd never get over it. Johnny and me, we go way back and I had to get away from my family and the disaster that was my life. I figured I'd lick my wounds and move on but you know what? I like it here. I think I might settle in Orca Bay."

"Unless an irate woman chases you out of town."

He looked at her very seriously. "Maybe that won't happen."

She wanted very badly to believe him, but both of their histories were in view. "Maybe."

He reached over and took her hand. "Can we do something?"

"I don't know, is it very kinky?"

He shook his head. "Let's pretend this is a real first date. Start from the beginning."

"Pretend you haven't seen me naked?"

He breathed slowly out, closing his eyes halfway. "Never going to happen. I'll try to put it out of my mind."

She said softly, "And if I tell you I'm not wearing any underwear, you can put that out of your mind, too."

This time he closed his eyes all the way, squeezed them shut in fact, then slowly opened them. It was as if he'd done some very quick Zen exercise and now returned to the present. "Is that how you show up to all your first dates?"

"Depends on the date."

"How am I going to survive tonight?"

It was fun to tease him, but the sad truth was she was turning herself on as relentlessly as she was arousing him. Maybe the no-underwear thing hadn't been her smartest move. But this dress showed everything, no panties she'd tried, not even the tiniest thong, worked. She felt her bare thighs sliding against each other when she crossed and uncrossed her legs, felt the fabric of her skirt against her butt and when she walked there were breezes where no breezes should be.

"What's the first thing you remember?" she asked him.

"The first thing I remember? Hmm, let's see. My dog, I guess. He was a black Lab, brilliantly named Blackie. I think he used to hang around me a lot. Protecting me probably, or nabbing my food when my mom wasn't looking. Why? Is there some profound psychological secret behind a person's first memory?"

"No. I was only trying to make the sort of conversation that will allow us to stay here and eat our dinner, not bolt to your place to have sex. And, since I was the one being provocative, I figured I should steer the conversation back to neutral waters." Interesting, though, that his first move after his fiancée dumped him was to go get a dog. She wished she didn't feel so sympathetic to him, or understand him quite so well.

"Are you really going commando?"

So much for safe conversational channels. "Yes."

"Then I hate to tell you this, but I think we're going to have to skip dessert."

She chuckled, low and dirty. "I am planning to be dessert."

He raised his hands in surrender. "Okay, your first memory?"

"Seeing my mama hang out the wash. I guess it was a windy day and I remember the sheets billowing." She closed her eyes briefly. "You know, I may have added some stuff, but I swear in that memory I can smell roses."

"There's a lot to learn from memory."

"I guess there is."

"Okay, this is good. We're doing great. How about your favorite day."

"Ever? In my whole life?"

"Yeah."

And somehow they talked like two normal people getting to know each other, or maybe getting to know each other in a different way. She found some new things about him. He was funnier than she thought. More conservative, too. The wine was gone, all the delicious food eaten and she realized maybe it hadn't been such a bad thing to take their relationship public after all. Natalie had left at some point, likely doing what Ben usually did. Catching a nap before the bartender/lover got home.

"You ready to go?"

"Yes."

On the way back to his place they didn't say much. He played with her hair, she ran her fingers up and down his thigh. When they burst through the door, they weren't as crazy horny as the first time they'd made love, but there was definitely an urgency there. They'd been concentrating on each other all evening, sharing secrets, bites of food, insights. No wonder dating tended to lead to sex. It was dangerous stuff.

Naturally, Buddy couldn't see her and not expect food, and naturally, she'd conned their waitress into putting a few beef scraps into a doggie bag. Ben pretended horror, while Buddy pretended nothing. His ecstasy was unfeigned. He raised one ear when they headed for the bedroom, but stayed near the front door sniffing around for any stray food.

Once inside Ben's bedroom, she started to peel off her dress when Ben stopped her. "No. Let me. Usually you climb in bed already naked. I want to undress you. I always miss that part."

So, she let him. He touched and stroked her as he removed her shoes and dress, making her melt. "You weren't kidding," he said, when he peeled her dress slowly up her thighs, revealing her nakedness.

"I wasn't kidding."

If that wasn't love in his eyes when he led her to the bed, it was something pretty damned close.

How had this happened to them? This new and wondrous thing?

She didn't think she'd ever made love or been made love to when there was so much love in the act. His kisses made her feel precious, his mouth and hands brought her to orgasm again and again before he finally entered her, surging inside of her as though he belonged.

They kept the lights on and their eyes open as they took each other, rolling and kissing, thrusting and easing off, making the magic last until they couldn't hold off any longer and they came together, still face-to-face, exposing themselves.

"I love you," he said.

A week ago, even a few days ago, she'd have scoffed at him, laughed it off. But she knew it was true even as the knowledge terrified her.

He kissed her gently and eased off her, clearly not expecting an answer.

She sat with the thrilling knowledge for a few minutes then whispered the truth that was in her heart. "I love you, too."

His voice was gruff but there was a note of appeal in his voice when he asked, "You staying the night?"

Another big step for her. "I brought my toothbrush."

"Good."

They made love twice more in the night, reaching for each other almost unconsciously. And when they weren't making love they slept curled around each other.

The phone woke her far too early.

"Whaat?" Her eyes opened and it took her a second to figure out where she was.

"What the hell?" A grumpy-sounding Ben reached across her for the phone beside the clock. Which read 7:10 a.m. "This better be a life-or-death emergency."

She bet it was work and was already pushing a pillow over her ear to block out the noise when he jerked to sitting, his whole body tensing.

"Sarah?"

Okay, now she was awake. "Sarah?" she echoed, stupidly. "*The* Sarah?"

He made a shushing motion with his hand, but the

tenseness in his body and the wild look in his eyes told her everything she needed to know.

Not willing to sit in his bed and eavesdrop while he talked to his ex on the phone, she got out of bed, strode naked to the bathroom, peed, washed her face and brushed her teeth and hair. Then she grabbed Ben's robe off the back of the door and stalked past him. He still had the wild-eyed look, but he made eye contact with her as she passed, rolling his eyes as if to say, what can I do?

Stumbling into the kitchen she found Buddy overjoyed to see her, his whole body wriggling and little happy squeals coming from his throat. Since he made it impossible to be in a bad mood, she got on the floor and played with him for a bit, then figured he probably needed to go outside.

The yard appeared to be fenced so she explained to him the importance of coming back then let him bound out the back door.

There was a sick, hollow feeling in her belly and she wished she hadn't agreed to spend the night, then she'd have been spared this awful situation. Ben seemed to have missed the little detail about how the ex phoned him for early chats.

Coffee. She needed coffee. A glance around the kitchen and she figured out where the coffee stuff was. Ben was clearly the logical, organized type. A stainless steel coffeemaker sat on the counter, in the cupboard above was everything she needed except the milk—in the fridge—and the coffee—in the freezer. The coffee was a rich, dark roast. At least he could do something right, she thought as she set it to brew.

She poured two cups, realized she had no idea how he liked his coffee. How was it she knew every spot on his body that was ticklish, but she had no idea how the man liked his coffee? It was a little sad.

She gave it to him black, carrying in a mug and setting it on the bedside table. He was still talking, in a low, soothing voice.

Whatever.

She took her own coffee outside to a small table where she sat and contemplated the interesting ups and downs her life had taken over the last twenty-four hours. Not so much a roller coaster, as a rocket that can't make up its mind whether to fly to Mars or crash to Earth.

A few minutes later, she heard Ben calling her name, a little frantically.

"Out here."

He came through the door and almost got knocked over as Buddy celebrated his arrival by launching himself at the man. Over his ecstatic doggy face her gaze connected with Ben's.

"I thought you'd left," he said.

"I didn't even think of it."

He ran a hand through his hair, making the morning spikes spikier. "That was Sarah."

"Yes. I heard."

He patted Buddy and then ambled over to sit across from her at the little table. "Her boyfriend went back to his wife."

She sipped her coffee, looked at the barbecue sitting at the side of the patio, how cozy it all was. "And now she wants you back."

He snorted. "Not going to happen." But he didn't

make eye contact. She was cynical enough, burned enough from the past, that she didn't think she believed him.

"Then why do you look like you're about to give me bad news?"

He blew out a breath. "She's a real mess, right now. I said I'd help her."

"Does this woman have no family? No friends? No one else she can call in her time of need?"

"Her family took my side when we broke up. Next to me, they were the most devastated. It was a horrible embarrassment for her father and mother. I don't think she has many friends. She was always a workaholic, and she had me."

"And she had you." She didn't know who was more pathetic. Ben for being such a fool, or her for—being such a fool.

"I'm going down there for a couple of days. Just to help her move into a new place." He shrugged. "She quit her job when he told her he was going back with his wife, and now she can't afford the rent."

"What a tragedy."

He glanced up at her. "This has nothing to do with you and me."

"Oh, Ben. It has everything to do with you and me. Sarah always did."

"Are you telling me not to go?"

She shook her head. "No. I wish she'd called twenty-four hours ago, that's all."

He got up, came around and knelt in front of her. "You have to trust me."

Unable to stop herself, she took his face in her hands

and kissed him gently. It wasn't his fault he was a fool for love, she supposed. "My trust has to be earned."

Then she got up and headed for the house.

"Where are you going?"

"You have to go play Sir Galahad. Which means it's time for me to leave."

18

Sexy Wiggles

1 oz strawberry schnapps
1 oz white rum
Ice cubes
Fill with 7-Up
Strawberries

Fill glass half full of ice. Add strawberry schnapps and rum. Fill glass the rest of the way full with 7-Up. Mix. Top glass off with whole strawberry.

HAD THOSE ROPES always hung there? Natalie wondered, almost slopping her morning coffee as she contemplated the coils hanging on the weathered siding. She was certain they'd been there all along; it was only that ever since Johnny had mentioned her and bondage in the same breath that she seemed to see straps, ties, ropes, and materials suitable for blindfolding purposes everywhere she looked at Johnny's place.

She had a pretty good idea he knew it, too.

"You like the rope? It's good and strong. You could

string up a hammock with that rope and it would easily take a man's weight."

"How interesting."

Then a little later he called, "Can you come in here and help me pick out a tie?"

"A tie? What do you need a tie for?" She'd never seen him wear one.

"I think I'm going to wear something more formal for the martini challenge next week. The outfit is part of the entire presentation, you know."

"But you haven't chosen a martini yet."

"Still, it's good to be prepared."

She walked into his bedroom and found him with his closet door open. He had to root behind the board shorts and Hawaiian shirts, the entire beach bartender wardrobe to access a rack full of ties.

"So many."

"I've picked them up here and there. I should get rid of some of them. I don't use them too often, but you never know when you're going to need a few ties." She looked up into his eyes and found them laughing at her, and that's when she realized he was deliberately torturing her.

He took one, a wide tie with a purple swirl on it, and held it out as if he was the Boston strangler and she was his next victim. "You should try one."

"I don't really wear ties." She took a step back and bumped into the bed. He took a step, followed her.

He looped the tie around the back of her neck and her nerve endings were so sensitive the stroke of the silk against her nape had a shiver running right down her spine.

"You should wear one, too, for the martini challenge."

And he knotted the tie and tightened it until the knot rested on her collarbone. "Nice." He nodded. "Now, follow me."

She wasn't sure about all this ordering around, but since he was going in the direction of the kitchen and away from the rest of the ties, she followed.

"What are we doing?" she asked, seeing him rummage around in the cupboard where he kept his booze.

"We are going to build a prizewinning cocktail."

"At ten in the morning?"

"You inspired me." His voice was muffled as he had stuck his head inside the cupboard and was rummaging around at the back, clanking bottles.

She shook her head. "Tying a tie around my neck inspired you?"

He rose in one smooth motion, two bottles in hand. "The inspiration is in removing the clothing. The reveal."

"It looks more to me like it's about getting drunk and naked at ten in the morning."

"That, too."

He was already busy with glasses and taking fruit from the fridge. In spite of herself, she was drawn forward. "What are you going to call it?"

He came around the counter, walked up to her and undid three buttons on her shirt, so her bra and a good bit of cleavage were visible. "The Striptini."

"You know I just got dressed."

"Sometimes you can be very rigid," he said reaching for another button.

She crossed her arms over her chest, stopping him in his tracks. "Maybe you should entice me with that drink, hmm?"

"Right. The drink." He backed off and she knew he'd already forgotten about mixing that drink. He was so easy.

"Right. The Striptini."

He mixed the ingredients.

"Oh, yes," she said on tasting it. "That's the winner, right there."

He sipped. Nodded. Seemed pleased, then his delight faded. "But how do we know it works?"

"Isn't it just supposed to taste good?"

"Does it make you want to take off your clothes?"

"Maybe I should have another sip."

"Another button."

He loved teasing her, loved the way her mouth went all prim even as the smile tugged to get free. Her hands were small, her nails sensibly short with only a layer of gloss to say they were polished. He watched, fascinated as she slipped a button free, revealing the mysterious shadow between her breasts. When she was finished, the tie slid back, covering the view.

She glanced at him and raised her brows. He passed her the drink, saw her take a sip. Lick her lips.

"Now, you."

"Me?"

She held the glass, more a dare than an offer. "A striptease works both ways."

He loved how sensible, and restrained and business-oriented she seemed, and yet how sexy she was the second you scratched the surface.

"I don't have any buttons on my shirt."

"Too bad. I guess the whole thing comes off, then."

He'd never, ever felt self-conscious undressing before a woman but as she observed him, the drink held in her hand, he found himself off balance a little. Weird.

Because he refused to think of this being weird, he took no time at all, just yanked the T-shirt over his head as though getting ready to jump into the shower.

There.

But he wasn't going for a shower, he was heading to paradise with a sweet, sexy woman, and the way her gaze lingered as it took in his naked chest and belly had him thinking this was going to be the fastest striptease in history.

He grabbed the glass. Took a sip. The flavor burst on his tongue, fruity but intense. Oh, he was good.

"What next?" she asked him. He could see her chest rising and falling, her nipples already prominent, giving her arousal away.

"Your shirt. The whole thing."

She didn't argue. He didn't think she wanted to drag this thing out, either. He would have thought they'd have slackened their urgency for each other by now, but if anything, he wanted her more every time he saw her.

Her fingers fumbled slightly as she undid the buttons she'd fastened not half an hour ago. He found her clumsiness, in such a tidy, efficient woman to be endearing.

Her skin was pale, the pale of Nordic ancestry and probably workaholic lifestyle. In a town where he saw so much tanned skin—and no amount of warning about the dangers of the sun ever seemed to stop California beach hounds—he found her paleness really, really sexy.

She took her sip. The drink was half-gone already.

"Now your pants."

"You don't waste time, do you?"

"I'm only glad you're not wearing socks."

Normally, he dragged his boxers off at the same time, but he needed to hang on to some clothing, so he peeled his jeans down slowly, making a bit of a show of it. He was so hard he didn't think he could hold out much longer.

He sipped, barely tasting the damn thing.

"Bra."

Reaching behind her slowly, she unfastened the clasp, then made a teasing show of holding on to the cups, before slowly letting the lacy underwear fall to the floor like a double snowflake.

The masculine tie hanging between her breasts nearly undid him. He'd only been teasing her with the thing, now it was teasing him, touching the skin he wanted to touch, filling his head with ideas—all the things a creative and very horny guy could do with a silk tie.

Naturally, he was one sip from naked and she was still half dressed, but he figured by the time that drink was gone, they'd be well primed.

His boxers were gone in no time, then her shoes, socks, jeans and panties. "I'll be drunk before I'm done," she complained.

"It's a good lesson not to wear so many clothes." He was enjoying the show. Sunlight spilled through the windows so the whole place was glowing. He loved this time of day.

When there was nothing but her tie left on her body, she drained the glass, then slowly unknotted the tie. There was a look in her eyes he didn't remember seeing before, determined, seductive.

In charge.

She approached him slowly, slipping the now-knotless tie from her neck, the ends toying with her breasts, then holding it very much the way he had when he'd first teased her with it. Taut, each end wrapped around one of her hands. Then she let go of one end, let it slide over her forearm. He was fascinated, watching her as though she were a snake charmer.

When she was in front of him, she took the tie and wrapped the length around his cock a few times. The sensation was exquisite, silky cool, and then she pulled on the other end and as the silk unwrapped itself from around his flesh he felt the pull, the slide.

"I was planning to tie you up with that," he croaked.

"Not right now. I need it."

She led him to the couch, pushed him until he flopped back, this time, slipped the tie around his balls and again he got the delicious feel of silk, pulling. Driving him crazy.

She went back to his penis. Again, dragged it out a little longer this time. Glorious torture.

"I can't take much more," he managed.

She wound the silk twice around the base of his cock and then tied a very neat, efficient bow. "That's my idea of bondage," she said, looking very pleased with herself. And she took everything above the ribbon into her mouth.

She drove him to the edge of madness until he couldn't take any more. He flipped her, so she was sitting on the couch, pulled her legs toward him, and plunged into her heat.

"The ribbon," she gasped.

"What about it?"

He thrust shallowly, quick, light thrusts, stopping himself each time the ribbon started to disappear.

Her head was back, her breasts arching as her passion built.

"The bow, it's rubbing me." She stopped on a gasp and he realized she'd unwittingly turned him into a sex toy.

Her legs wrapped tight around him, she started to buck helplessly and then she wailed as the orgasm swamped her.

He plucked and tugged at the ribbon before finally getting it off, slipped a condom on with a lot more haste than finesse. She was panting, staring up at him with wide, dilated eyes. "Hurry."

After that, nothing could hold him back. This time he thrust in all the way, reaching deep, as deep as he could go and always wanting more. She twisted her hips, jerking against him and he helped her along with his finger between them replacing the knot of the ribbon. He barely managed to wait for her, and when he felt her body clench and milk him, when he came, he felt as if a dam had burst.

Then he did the oddest thing. He picked her up and carried her to his bed, where he wanted nothing more than to simply hold her for a while.

They were both drifting, catching a little nap before the next round, when there came a banging on the front door.

Not a friendly, neighborly knock, either, it sounded as though somebody was using their fist like a battering ram.

"Is someone at the door?" Natalie asked him drowsily.

"That is the sound of bad energy trying to get into my space. We'll ignore them."

"Good plan." She smiled against his shoulder. "You are so new age."

"And what are you? Old age?"

She thumped him. Naturally he retaliated, which was leading nicely to round two when Natalie screamed.

"What the—"

He looked up to the ever-open doors to his bedroom. There, silhouetted against the morning sun was a woman.

And not just any woman.

"What are you doing here, Rita?"

"Sorry to barge in on you like this," she said, sounding anything but—there was no room inside that woman for anything but anger.

"Why aren't you with Ben?"

"That's what I wanted to talk to you about."

"Okay." He shifted to his back. He'd never turned away a friend in trouble, didn't plan to start now. "What's up?"

"Um…" Natalie had the sheet pulled up to her chin and looked less than comfortable. "Maybe you could go in the kitchen and brew some coffee. We'll be right out."

Suddenly a flicker of amusement crossed Rita's face, making her a lot more recognizable. "You go ahead and finish up. Don't mind me. I'll wait in the kitchen."

"We weren't—" Natalie began, all flustered, but Rita only laughed.

"How do you like your coffee?"

19

Bikinitini

3 oz vodka
1 oz orange liqueur
1 oz fresh lemon juice
1/2 cup cucumber, peeled and seeded, cut into
chunks
Fresh mint leaves

In blender combine all ingredients except mint.
Process until slushy. Serve in martini glass,
garnish with mint.

"SARAH?" Natalie could not believe what she was
hearing. "Sarah was on the phone at seven in the
morning? The first night you sleep over?"

"Yep. Sarah, the woman who dumped him two
weeks before the wedding. Sarah, the woman he left
San Francisco to escape. Sarah, the home wrecker who
got her married lover to leave his wife and three kids
for her."

"What did she want?" Johnny asked abruptly.

"You mean, what did she say she wanted or what did
she really want?"

"It's too early for analysis. Can I just have what she said she wanted? Let's start there."

"Her married boss boyfriend dumped her and she wants Ben to help her move."

Johnny had been sitting on the couch with his coffee, but at that, he leaped up. "Yes. Justice is served. She got dumped." Then he made laughing sounds like a crazy person and did what looked like a Native American war dance. Or maybe it was his own crazy jig.

"Is he going to do it?"

Natalie figured she had the answer since Rita was here, but she felt she needed to gather all the relevant facts.

"Oh, yeah. He's going to do it."

Johnny's dance stopped midstep. He had a leg raised as though he were attempting to knee himself in the groin. "He's going? To help that bitch move?"

"That's what he told me."

"She put him through the grinder. She destroyed him. Why would he help her?"

"Now we get to what she really wants. That woman wants him back," Rita said with a bitter flourish.

"You don't know that," Natalie said.

"Why else would she call him? Of all people? Call a moving company if you want to move. You don't call your former fiancé."

Johnny shook his head firmly. "Ben would never go back to her."

"I hadn't even got my shoes on when he'd started packing for his road trip."

"That's crazy. He doesn't want her."

"He wants you," Natalie finished. She placed her hand over Rita's. "You know he does."

To everyone's surprise, Rita's eyes teared up. "He told me he loved me."

Joy filled Natalie's heart. She felt a little misty herself. "He did?"

Rita nodded, dabbing at her lower lids with a red-tipped finger. "Last night. I finally let him convince me to go out with him and look what happens."

"You love each other, you'll work it out." It was as though her eyes had a will of their own—quite inde-pendent of her, they looked over at Johnny and she dis-covered that he was gazing at her just as intently.

Her heart felt tight in her chest. She glanced away quickly, but the shared moment was as blinding as any words could ever be.

She loved him.

Maybe he even loved her, too.

Which was about the stupidest thing to ever have happened. What could they possibly do about it? They lived half a country away from each other, and their styles, personalities, what they wanted from life, were all so very different that it was ridiculous to even con-template a future beyond next week.

And yet, a tiny, teeny, voice whispered to her. And yet. Maybe the impossible was possible.

Maybe one of them could change.

She thought of introducing Johnny to some of her colleagues and wondered what they'd talk about. Then chastised herself for being a snob. She was equally out of her element in his world, but she was managing. In fact, more than managing. She'd made a friend, some-thing she didn't have a whole heap of.

And her friend was in trouble, she reminded herself,

forcing her thoughts away from her own dilemma and back to Rita's.

"So, how did you leave Ben?"

"Exactly like that. I left Ben."

"But not—"

"I'm not going to fight, I'm not going to yell, and I'm not going to beg." She bared her teeth on the last word. "I tried all that once and it didn't work out so well. If he wants me, the man knows where to find me. He drove me home and we didn't have too much to say to each other. Then he left and I didn't know what to do with myself. I got madder and madder, and then I got in the car and drove here. Impulsive, I guess."

"I can't believe he's going. Sarah, she's—all wrong for him. He's changed. He's not the man he was when he knew her. He came here and made himself a different life. He likes it. Why would he go back to the rat race and follow the rules of a traditional lifestyle that he fled?" Johnny shook his head, more she thought as though trying to convince himself. "It doesn't make sense."

"Besides," she said, trying to bring the topic back to Rita's heartache, "He loves you."

"Well, I guess we'll find out." She dropped her head back against the sofa cushions. "Sorry I broke in on you like this. I had to talk to someone or I would have gone crazy."

"No. It's good that you did."

Rita's gaze took in the clothing scattered around the room, the drink makings still out on the counter. Natalie hoped she didn't notice the snake of silk tie peeking out from under the couch.

"It's a good thing I didn't arrive half an hour earlier."

Natalie blushed deeply. Johnny laughed.

A dog came bounding in.

Tongue hanging out, tail wagging, the big golden Lab looked at the three people then let out a woof and ran to Rita and laid his head in her lap.

"Buddy." She sounded happy to see him even as her eyes narrowed and she glared at the open door. Sure enough, Buddy's owner was there.

"I should go," Rita said, putting her coffee mug down with a snap and standing.

"No," Ben said. "I saw your car out front. Rita, I was looking for you."

She looked pugnacious as she faced him. "Well, you found me."

"I want to ask you something."

Natalie didn't even realize she'd moved closer to Johnny until she felt his hand around hers.

"What?"

"Will you look after Buddy while I'm gone?"

On hearing his name, the dog wagged his tail, looking from Ben to Rita and back again as if he knew something was up.

"You want me to look after your dog while you move your old girlfriend?"

"Yes. Yes, I do."

Johnny shifted restlessly beside her. She knew he was about to blurt that he'd look after the dog, so she squeezed his hand in warning.

Rita's arms wrapped around herself, as though she had a bad stomachache and was about to double over, but she remained upright. She looked down at Buddy, who was still wagging his tail. "Yeah. I'll look after your dog. But why do you have to go?"

"Because it's the right thing to do."

If anyone wanted Natalie's opinion, it was a stupid-ass thing to do, and she was pretty sure that Johnny and Rita would back her up on that. But Ben plainly operated from his own code of behavior and, right or wrong, she found she respected that he'd do what he thought was right.

She only hoped the irresistible Sarah had lost her power over him.

Ben walked over to Rita. Handed her a piece of paper. "I'm staying at my parents' place if you need me. Here's the number."

She stared at him. "Your parents' house?"

"Yes." He kissed her hard. "Trust me."

She didn't speak, only nodded silently.

"Come on back to my place. I'll show you what Buddy needs."

When they had left, Natalie scampered to pick up all the discarded clothing, horrified at what Rita and Ben had seen, while Johnny looked frowningly at the contents of his Striptini laid out all over the counter. "Do you think she could tell what I put in the drink?" he asked her.

She stopped to kiss him swiftly. "I think she had other things on her mind."

"You can never tell. She's a very crafty woman, that Rita."

"Tell me something. Is she crazy or is he?"

"You ask me, we all are."

She laughed. "Well, we certainly are. But it's a good kind of crazy."

She finished putting the clothes away and made the bed in case they had any more visitors barging right into the bedroom that day. When she came out, Johnny said, "Oh, I forgot to tell you, I did something I hope you'll like."

"What?"

"I traded shifts so I can work days next week until you leave. We'll have more time together. They're shorter shifts, too." He grinned at her. "Make sure you get your sleep. You're going to need the extra stamina."

She was delighted and horrified at the same time.

"But—"

"What? Don't you want to spend more time together?"

"Of course, I do. It's you I'm worried about. Should you give up hours? What about the money you're losing?"

He turned his back on her to put the liquor back in the cupboard, and when he faced her there was an odd expression on his face. As if she'd let him down in some way. "Money is a big issue for you, isn't it?"

She opened her mouth. Closed it. Couldn't even figure out how to answer that. Finally she said, "Yes. It's huge. Money's important, Johnny. It's how we buy things, save for big goals." She felt she was explaining something that people like Johnny sometimes missed learning. "Your lifestyle here—" she waved a hand around everything she could see "—it's great when you're young and fancy-free, but don't you want things? Don't you have goals for the future?"

He rubbed his chin as though giving the matter serious thought. "Well, I'd like to surf in Australia again. That was amazing. Maybe get a second bike, but what do I need that I don't have?"

"You're smart and personable. You could do so much."

"Like what?"

"I don't know. Don't you have dreams? Goals? Maybe a new career you might like to try?"

"I like bartending. It suits me. I'm good at it."

"But what about building something for the future?"

A tiny frown formed between his eyebrows. It was so unusual to see a frown there that it made her realize how happy he usually was. "What if I owned my own bar? Or a restaurant? Would that make me more acceptable to you?"

She heard the edge in his voice. "Johnny, you're completely acceptable to me. I'm thinking of you, that's all. How long can you go on like this, renting a house, owning almost nothing. Don't you want a future?"

"Like you have, you mean? I should go to school for a bunch of years and then spend my life in offices? Working so many hours I never see the sunshine? You think that's such a great life?"

She was so frustrated, she didn't even understand why. She'd been careful not to mock his lifestyle, and he was seriously mocking hers. "You can't be a kid forever, playing on your surfboard and riding your bike. Someday you have to grow up."

"Why do you care? You won't be here. Next week, you'll be gone."

She stalked to the window and stared out. Why did she care so much? He was right. If he wanted to laze away his life, it was no business of hers.

The truth stared back at her like a reflection. "Because I care about you," she said softly.

"So would it?"

"Would it what?"

"Make a difference if I owned the restaurant?"

She turned back to him. "Is that something you really want to do? You'd need to raise some capital, prepare a business plan. I could help you with all of that. If it's what you really want."

"It isn't. I'm trying to figure out whether it's the business or the fact that I'm only a lowly server that really bugs you?"

She took a step toward him. "That's not fair. I'm only trying to help you."

"I'm the one who sleeps like a baby, who has no stress. I surf when I feel like it, take a vacation when I want one. You toss in your sleep and sometimes you wake me up with the sound of your teeth grinding. You wear your stress like a designer suit. Are you sure your life is so much better?"

Stress was so much a part of her life, she barely noticed it anymore except when it was temporarily missing, like most of the time when she was with Johnny. "Maybe not. I only want—"

"We don't all want to run corporate America."

"No. I guess you're right. It was foolish of me. I guess Ben and Rita got to me." She thought about stopping there and decided, screw it, maybe it was time to tell him honestly how she felt. "They've been apart because they were both too stubborn to admit their feelings, too stubborn to try and change. And I thought, do I really want to walk away from this man?"

He gulped. She saw his Adam's apple bob up and down.

She let out a nervous giggle. "Oh, God. Now I've made you panic. It's okay. Forget I started this stupid topic."

"No. I want to know the answer to your question. Do you want to walk away?"

She shook her head. She spoke quickly so she wouldn't lose her nerve. "I own an apartment in Chicago. I have so many contacts there. You could come and stay with me for a while, I could help you get set up. You could go to school if you wanted to—"

"I already have a degree."

Her shock was probably evident. "You do?"

"Yes. Environmental studies with a minor in ocean-ography."

"Oh. Well, that's great. Having a degree says a lot about you. That you can finish things, that you're moti-vated and intelligent. In Chicago, you could really go places. You could even bring your sailboat."

"Tough to surf, though."

She blew out a breath. "You don't have any inten-tion of coming to Chicago. Forget I brought it up, it was a stupid idea." She felt utterly foolish, having made her feelings for him so clear. She was offering everything she had. Her home, her contacts, her re-sources and her heart. He apparently wasn't interested in any of them. She looked down at her toes, bare, which was very unlike her. With the Rita invasion she'd scrambled into clothes and hadn't bothered with socks or shoes.

"Can I have a turn now?" His voice was gentle, loving even.

She nodded, still looking down at her feet.

His equally bare feet came into her line of vision as he neared. They were weather-beaten and tough as an old sailor's next to her lily-white toes with the delicate pink polish. Even their feet gave away how utterly unlike they were.

He put a hand under her chin and lifted her face until she was looking at him.

"I care about you, too," he said. "I don't think either of us had any clue this thing would get so serious so fast."

Well, at least he was admitting he had feelings, too; that was something. She shook her head, as shocked as he was that she'd fallen hard and fast for a guy who was supposed to be a harmless fling.

"I want to ask you something. Don't answer right now, but think about it. If money was no object. If you had all you'd ever want and I had all I'd ever want, where would you choose to live? Here on the beach or in your apartment in Chicago?"

"That's not fair, it's a completely hypothetical—"

He put two fingers over her lips and the gesture shocked her to silence.

"I asked you to think about it. Don't give me a gut reaction about what's not fair. I want an honest answer."

He removed his hand so she could say, "Why? What would the purpose be?"

"Because, my darling bean counter, there are always options in life."

Orca Bay was undeniably beautiful and the lifestyle was relaxed and more fun than ought to be legal, but what was he suggesting? That she get a waitress job so they had the same shifts and could surf and play together? She, with her MBA?

He was looking at her as though he understood her all too well.

"You could move in here." He paused. Swallowed again. "I've never offered that to any woman. Never wanted to."

"I—I…"

"Natalie, I think I'm in love with you."

20

Blue Sky Martini

2 1/2 oz vodka
1/4 oz blue curaçao
Splash of lime mix

Shake and strain over ice.
Rim glass with sugar.

TYPICAL MAN, she thought. He wanted her to give up everything. Her job, her home, her city. He didn't have to change a thing. No sacrifices required.

Well, he might be Hot Johnny, but he wasn't that hot.

He loved her. He'd said it. *He loved her!*

Sitting on the beach was one of the greatest places to seriously think, she'd discovered. It was unlike her to be so still, but somehow sitting here and watching the waves seemed like exactly the right thing to do.

And almost as though whispering the truth, the waves seemed to say, he's giving up his freedom.

The man whom Rita had warned her never committed to anything long term was offering her his freedom. And his love.

But were they enough?

By unspoken agreement, she and Johnny didn't talk about the future. They'd both said their pieces, she was thinking about his very odd question, and they were definitely making the most of every second they had together. Sailing, making love, laughing, making love… He was even attempting to teach her to surf, which led to more laughing, more lovemaking.

Even though she was working hard and efficiently at the Hennington, she felt as though she were on holiday. She'd never had so much fun. Or found someone who suited her so well. Even though they didn't have much in common, it seemed they had a connection unlike any she'd ever known. They laughed at the same things, shared core values. She was surprised, when she scratched the surface of his easygoing lifestyle to find that he had some traditional ideas that coincided with hers.

Even his earring was growing on her.

Rita and she took Buddy for a long walk together every day and alternately ranted and moaned about the men they'd been crazy enough to love. Ben was due home Friday, or so he said. Even though he phoned Rita every night and insisted he loved her and no longer had any feelings for Sarah except a little pity, Natalie knew that Rita wouldn't relax until he was back. "On his knees, begging my forgiveness," was how she put it.

When she told Rita about Johnny's odd question, the woman laughed. "Money or happiness. Why do you always have to pick one? Can't a woman have both?"

"Yes, but you have to work hard. Sacrifice in the early years, build a foundation. But Johnny doesn't see it that way."

Friday, the day of the martini challenge, dawned. He wouldn't be going in to work until later, and she had to get to the lodge, so she left him sleeping, thinking that she'd never had more fun doing a job, or wanted less to return home and get back to her regular routines.

The lodge was always quietest in the mornings. She had her own temporary desk in the administration offices in the oldest part of the hotel and she'd come in today mostly to tidy up some loose ends. She'd completed all her research, already made some suggestions and seen some new systems implemented.

She'd be back in a couple of months with a final report and hopefully, within six months, the profit margins would show an increase. She was positive they would.

Along with the sadness of leaving was the satisfaction she received from helping fix an ailing company. And the lodge particularly appealed to her, somehow. She'd made friends here. She wanted this place to succeed.

When the general manager of the hotel, Otto Schrieben, called her into his office, she slipped on her suit jacket, and entered the large space. Filled with dark wood and a massive mahogany desk, it was an office where no computer found a home. If Otto wanted to send a letter or a memo, he called in his secretary and dictated his needs.

He rose when she came in. A courtly gentleman with the slightest German accent, he'd lived all around the world running hotels and landed here. He was sixty, and she suspected he'd remain here until he retired.

"Natalie, please sit down."

"Thank you."

She took a seat in the leather club chair and waited.

"Will you have some coffee? I usually have some at this time."

"Thank you."

Since she already knew all his routines, she wasn't a bit surprised to see a tray of coffee in a silver pot with the hotel china, sugar and real cream.

Once they were sipping their coffees, he said, "And how have you enjoyed your time here in Orca Bay? You've caught some sun, I see, and look very much more relaxed, if I may say so, than when you arrived."

Had her stress level been that obvious? How had she not even known it? "I love it here," she said. "And the hotel has been a wonderful project for me. The staff were helpful and I'm confident we can improve the bottom line quite a bit."

"I will admit I was a trifle hesitant to hire you, but the owners insisted. I've been pleased by what a difference you've made in a short time. You seem able to see things that others miss."

She smiled. It wasn't the first time she'd heard those words. "It's because I'm an outsider. I've no preconceived notions or expectations. I can think creatively. That's how I work best."

"And you never once insisted I get a computer, which we both know would be much more efficient."

He was twinkling at her.

"I respect how you operate. And you and Margaret are a very efficient team. You have no interest in learning the computer. Why would I want you to waste so much of your time learning something you despise? That would be counterproductive."

"You are a realist. I like that."

"Thank you."

He placed his coffee cup on his saucer. Looked over the big desk at her. "I had a conference call with the owners yesterday. They met you, of course, before they hired your firm."

She nodded.

"And I was very happy to be able to give them a glowing report of all you've accomplished here."

"Thank you."

He dipped his head. "They suggested a bonus. I suggested we offer you a job." He leaned back and patted his ample belly as though making sure all his buttons were buttoned, which they were. "I would like to offer you the position of executive manager of the hotel. You would be my second in command."

Her eyes widened slightly. This was a great job—if a person wanted to work in the hotel business.

And stay in Orca Bay.

"I'm flattered."

"I would train you in the specific aspects of the hotel business. Indeed, I would hope to train you to be my successor one day." He looked up at her. "Of course, you would have to commit to stay for at least five years."

"I see."

She'd been offered a number of jobs and never had she been even slightly tempted. But this one had her jumping with excitement. It was entirely due to the challenge the job presented, she told herself.

Well, almost entirely.

"May I think about this and let you know tomorrow?"

"Of course, my dear. Sleep on it. Talk it over

with…whoever you need to. I very much hope your answer will be yes."

"I am truly tempted." She rose. "And I really am grateful to you. I'll let you know tomorrow."

"Fine. Take the rest of the day. Walk along the beach, think about what you really want. It's what I do when I'm puzzling over something."

As she left the meeting, her head was whirling with ideas and possibilities. She'd never been the sort of woman who could imagine herself giving up a job and moving to a new city for a man. When Frederick had moved she'd never seriously considered going with him, even though she'd known it meant the end of their relationship.

So why, now, was she considering doing that very thing for a surf bum whose biggest commitment was that he was willing to let her move in with him?

It seemed she wanted more.

She knew Johnny was ready for the challenge tonight when the Striptini would be unveiled. It had been her idea to get a pole and pole dancers at the booth, and, naturally, Johnny already knew a couple of dancers he could call up. How he knew them she didn't think she wanted to know.

She had indeed been his muse, helping design a simple gauzy cover that you had to open to get to the drink itself, which was completely delicious and she was certain would win. She'd left him sleeping when she came in to work today, where she assumed she'd find him still.

She'd already decided to stay the weekend, and then on Sunday night she was booked to fly back to Chicago. Now she wasn't so sure she was going.

Normally she was so orderly, organized, predictable. But, at the moment, she felt confused, scared, elated, loving and loved, and then by turns foolish and fooled.

This was insane.

She didn't even bother to go to her room and change first, she headed straight for her rental car, knowing it wasn't a walk on the beach that she needed right now, it was some straight talk with the man she'd fallen in love with.

It was easy to talk of love and throw out ideas for staying together, but now she had an actual job offer, she needed to know that the man she was willing to make this huge change for actually wanted her.

She was nervous when she got to his place. He wasn't sleeping, as she'd imagined, but sitting on his back deck, one of his favorite spots, drinking orange juice and reading the paper.

Over the noise of the surf he hadn't heard her approach so she had a moment to watch him and she knew that he was, for her, the forever kind of love.

When she came near, he looked up, his eyes lighting the way they did when he saw her.

He got out of his seat and kissed her. "Hey, nice suit. Makes me want to peel it off you."

Even as lust surged through her, she shook her head. "I didn't come here for sex."

"Then you came to the wrong place."

He pulled out a chair for her, and sat back down, obviously getting that there was something going on or she wouldn't have shown up not two hours after she'd left.

She sat down. Stood up again. Didn't have a clue how to say what she needed to say, where even to begin.

"Natalie, what is it?"

When she heard the concern in his voice, she thought she wanted to be with him so badly she was almost willing to be the one making all the changes, all the sacrifices. But even so, she needed to know that he loved her enough.

"I got offered a job today."

"Really? What sort of job?"

"A good job. A really, really good job. Here in Orca Bay."

She studied him carefully as she spoke and realized there was no way he could have faked that easy delight. There wasn't even a nanosecond's pause. "That's fantastic. So, you'll stay? I mean, you'll take the job, right?"

Now came the hard part. "I said I'd think about it. But a lot of my answer will depend on you."

Some of his delight faded. He folded the paper and pushed it away as though the breeze rustling the pages was bothering him. "Natalie, I love you. But I am who I am. If you love me, you'll accept that. I'm never going to take some junior management training course, or open my own restaurant, not even for you."

She smiled a little. "I can't believe I ever asked that of you. I know that. I don't care." And she felt the truth of those words as she spoke them. He was her polar opposite in so many ways, which was probably one of the reasons he made her so happy. She was a Type A to the core; he was a Type B through and through. She was a workaholic; he put play and relaxation first. She scheduled; he liked spontaneity. She lived mostly in her head; he lived in his body. She lived in the future, always planning ahead; he lived in the now.

And somehow, their differences were rubbing off on each other. She was suddenly ready to work for one company, making a difference, rather than parachuting in, analyzing, diagnosing, fixing and then flying off to another troubled company. She was ready, she realized, to settle.

She thought maybe she'd be good for him, too. She challenged him, she thought, made him plan ahead a little bit, even as he helped her to relax. Not that she wanted to look that far ahead, but she absolutely knew he'd be the type of father who'd be only too happy to take care of the kids when she had to work.

"The thing is, I am in this thing all the way, and I'm proving it to you by giving up my entire life to move here."

"You're saying it's me, not the job?"

"It's both. But if I'm brutally honest, it's you first, then the job."

He took her hand. "I hope it will always be me first and then the job."

A feeling of possibility stole through her. "I think it always will be."

"So, what's bothering you? Why aren't we popping a champagne cork right now and celebrating?"

"I need to know that you love me enough."

"Enough for what? You can't quantify love—it won't fit on one of your spreadsheets. You can't analyze it in a report. You have to trust it."

"But I'm giving you proof that I love you."

"You want proof that I love you? That's crazy. I'm giving you everything I've got. I want us to be together. How much more proof do you want?"

"I can't explain it, but I'll always wonder, I think.

What if I'd gone back to Chicago? Would we have even tried to make this work?"

"You know we would. I was already talking about coming out later in the spring. It wouldn't be easy, but we could figure out a long-distance relationship. This is a lot better, though."

He held both her hands now, a little tighter than he usually did. "I asked you a question that you still haven't answered."

"If money was no object, where would I choose to live? I know. At the time I thought it was a dumb question, because money is always an issue. But now we can have both. I'll get a good salary, probably less than I make now with bonuses, but that's okay. It will be plenty for us to live on."

"You won't miss your fancy lifestyle and your MBA boyfriends?"

"Maybe once in a while I'll feel like flying to Paris to go shopping and remember that we can't do it." She shrugged. "If I ever get that way, you'll have to take me in the bedroom and remind me of all the reasons I don't need to go to Paris shopping. Other than that, we'll be fine. I'll sell my apartment in Chicago. I've got some money saved."

"You won't be embarrassed to be with a guy who is happy to be a bartender and never wants to be CEO of anything?"

"I love you. If you're a bartender, I love a bartender. If you decide to do something else, I'll love that, too. I honestly never thought I'd end up with someone like you. Maybe that's why I was never this happy before."

He pulled her right off the seat and kissed her so passionately there was no room for doubt.

"You know, we could even make some changes to the house if you want to."

"Changes? You mean like paint the walls?"

He was giving her that strange, half-amused look, as if he was having a private joke at her expense. Since she was spilling her guts here, telling him how much she loved him, it seemed a little inappropriate. "I mean, extend the house if we need to. Make it bigger."

"And why would you spend a lot of money on a house that doesn't belong to you."

"Because it does belong to me."

"What did you say?" The ocean was making so much noise she couldn't even hear straight anymore.

"Natalie, I own this house. Have done for years. I'm not a bum. I just don't have big career aspirations."

"You own this place?"

"Yes."

She looked around at the dock, the beach, the amount of land. "How do you even manage the mortgage? It must be huge."

"The taxes are bad enough. There is no mortgage. I paid that off as fast as I could." He grinned at her. "I worked a lot harder for a few years. I wasn't always the slacker you see before you."

She couldn't believe it; in her experience there was a certain path a person followed to be successful. Hanging out on the beach, slinging martinis and surfing weren't part of the program. "Is this a practical joke?"

"Do you want to see the property deed?"

"Oh, my God. You're serious. Do you have any idea what this property is worth?"

"Yes."

She pulled a hand away from his so she could put it over her heart. "I don't believe it. Why didn't you tell me?"

"I don't usually waste a lot of time talking about my possessions. They are completely irrelevant to who I am. It was mostly a fluke, anyway. I've never wanted a lot of stuff or been a huge partier, so I always had extra money. It added up and when this place came up for sale I was able to buy it."

"You own beachfront property in California."

"I also own an apartment building," he said, almost apologetically.

Her eyes narrowed. Everything was upside down today. "What's your net worth?"

He named a figure and her eyes widened. "You're worth more than I am."

"Guess those shopping trips to Paris won't be a problem then."

Somehow she doubted she was going to need them anymore. She thought lazy weekends sailing and barbecues on the back deck with friends would be a lot more fun.

Against all odds, she seemed to have bagged herself a rich man. She should be delighted.

If only she could rid herself of the nagging worry that he might not be as totally committed to this relationship as she was. Still, what was the worst that could happen? She'd make a fool of herself and end up brokenhearted and looking for a new job.

Big deal.

He tapped her lightly on the nose. "You've got a strange look on your face. Why do I feel like I'm supposed to do something, make some grand gesture?"

"A grand gesture would definitely help. Like when Rita agreed to be seen in public with Ben. It was her way of saying out loud that she was with him."

"I could do that. I could take you out for dinner."

"Not quite the same issue, with us, is it?"

"In a way it is. It's about trust."

21

Love in a Glass

1 1/2 oz raspberry liqueur
2 dashes Amaretto
1 1/2 oz vodka
1 oz sour mix

Mix in a shaker, pour into a cordial glass.

THE MARTINI CHALLENGE was held in a community center: Johnny had explained it was so that none of the competing venues would have an unfair advantage. She supposed that was a reasonable explanation for not holding the challenge in a proper bar or restaurant, but it was a little strange walking into a gymnasium-size building that had a stage and huge sprung floor. You could imagine a night of square dancing here or an amateur theatrical production.

However, the committee had done an amazing job of transforming a rather bland space into a one-night-only cocktail lounge. Colored balloons and streamers gave a festive air; the round tables were covered with white cloths, and there was a dance floor, a sound system and about twenty stations set up, each showcasing a single cocktail.

Every patron was given a scoring card and the idea was to wander from station to station, receive a small drink sample and evaluate the drink based on taste, of course, but also color, garnish and there were even marks for how creatively the booth was decorated and the bartenders costumed.

She was trying to decide whether to start at the beginning and work her way around, in an orderly fashion, to Johnny's station, or follow her desire and go straight to his, when Rita came rushing up to her. It took her a second to recognize her friend since the woman wore a gauzy, golden, togalike robe and her face and shoulders were painted gold.

"Wow."

"Oh, yeah. My drink's called Gold Zinger. It's got flakes of 24 karat gold floating on top. But who cares about that? Have you seen Ben? Or heard from him?" Creases of worry were digging golden creases into her forehead.

Natalie shook her head, realizing she'd been so wrapped up in her own love dilemma that she hadn't had time to worry about Rita's.

"He was supposed to fly in this afternoon. He didn't call." Rita grabbed her, her gold-colored nails leaving marks as she clutched at her arms. "Natalie, I love him. What if he doesn't come back? What if he stayed with Sarah? What if he breaks my heart? What if—"

"What if you turn around and look behind you?"

Her eyes widened, hope dawning when she saw Natalie's smile. For a second they stood absolutely still and then Rita turned. Ben was behind her, in a formal suit and tie that made him look like an elegant stranger, carrying a bouquet that needed a little work. Natalie wasn't sure what he'd been thinking. It wasn't as if the man couldn't afford to go to a florist. In his arms were roses, at least three dozen, but they weren't proper florist roses. They looked as though they came out of someone's garden. Several someones. There were a rainbow of colors, different varieties of roses, and some of the stems were crooked.

But Rita didn't seem to mind. She took one look at the bouquet and cried out, "Mama's roses." Which indicated to Natalie that Ben knew more about what Rita liked than she did.

Rita launched herself into his arms and he quickly held the huge bouquet of roses to the side before she impaled herself on the thorns, and hugged her tight with one arm. He was going to end up with his Armani suit gilded, but he didn't seem to care.

"You came back," Rita cried.

"I told you I would. It was you from the moment I met you. It will always be you."

Realizing she was staring, and that this was a very private moment, Natalie turned away, feeling a lump in her throat.

She looked down at her scorecard, but the words swam. She needed to sit down. No, go for a run. No, maybe dance, or sing really loud, bad karaoke. Maybe she just needed to find her guy.

In the end, she realized, there were no grand gestures or evidence that could prove a person's love. You gave them yours, fully and completely, and trusted they loved you in return.

As epiphanies went, she didn't think it was a bad one. She thought she'd find Johnny and tell him she didn't need grand gestures. She only needed him.

She didn't realize she'd stumbled toward a booth until a voice said, "You want to try a Salty Mermaid?"

"No thanks, I'm having an epiphany."

"I didn't see that on the list. Anyhow, you should try the mermaid."

"Okay, thanks." She took the drink, but didn't even want it. The booth was cute, though, decorated with an underwater theme, and the salt rim on the glass was a nice touch. When she sipped the drink she had to agree it was good, though not as good as Johnny's. The waitresses were dressed in sequined bikini tops, of course, and fake tails.

"Do you know where the Striptini booth is?"

"Where are you getting these names from? That's not on the list, either."

"It must be. The Driftwood?"

"Driftwood's in the corner over there. They aren't serving a Striptini, though."

"But—" She'd lost the woman's attention as two more guests had arrived to try the drink. Natalie moved on, giving her barely touched drink to a passing busboy.

As she searched out Johnny's booth, she thought there must be a mistake on the program. The corner where the Driftwood should be didn't have a pole and pole dancers, the colors weren't even right. Instead of blue tones, the booth was pink.

Really, really pink. Pink like the Valentine's day decorations from the first day she'd met Johnny.

She was about to keep looking when she saw Johnny himself. Not in the tight pants and leather jacket they'd chosen. He was wearing a tuxedo. And, if she wasn't mistaken, he'd had his hair cut and styled.

She walked up to the booth, feeling completely confused. A small crowd had gathered around the booth. Behind the table, the female servers wore bright fuchsia dresses that reminded her of bridesmaid gowns and the guys all wore tuxes.

His face lit up when he saw her. She was certain she hadn't imagined that. She was pretty sure her own expression mirrored his. In spite of the crowd and the fact that he was working, he drew her close and kissed her. "Hi."

"Hi." She felt as foolish as a twelve year old with her first boy crush.

"What is going on?" she asked him, pulling herself together with an effort. "Where's the Striptini."

"Change of plan. I invented a new cocktail today. In your honor."

A funny feeling like effervescence began to bubble inside of her. "In my honor? You did? What's it called? The Natalie?"

"It's called, True Love."

"Oh, Johnny."

He motioned to one of his helpers to take over, grabbed two martini glasses that had some pink liquor in them and reached behind him for a dark glass champagne bottle. "The secret ingredient is vintage champagne. But only you get that. Everyone else gets ordinary bubbly."

He took her hand and led her out through one of the doors and into the evening. There was a kids' playground with a picnic table a little away from the main building and he took her there.

After seating her at the picnic table, he opened the champagne cork with a flourish and poured the bubbling wine into their glasses.

He handed her one of the glasses and raised his own. "A toast. To true love."

"True love," she echoed.

"Oh, my." She sipped and the drink blended perfectly with what she was feeling. "You know what's weird? I just had an epiphany. Ben showed up with a bunch of roses that looked like they were handpicked out of someone's garden, and Rita yelled, 'Mama's roses,' which I guess means something special to them. And then it hit me. I don't need a grand gesture. I only need to love you and trust that you love me back."

He looked dumbfounded. "You mean I sacrificed my chance of winning the competition for nothing?"

"Of course you haven't sacrificed the competition. This drink is delicious. One of the best martinis I've ever tasted in my life."

"First, it's not a real martini since there's no vodka or gin in it, so that disqualifies my invention right there. Second, it's a total chick drink. No guy would vote for this concoction, even if it wasn't already disqualified."

She took another sip, wondering if all these bubbles were going to her head. She didn't feel anything like herself. "You mean it's—"

He nodded. "Grand gesture, baby. Grand gesture. Now you say you didn't need one after all?"

"Well, maybe I didn't need it, but it's awfully nice to get one."

As she raised her glass to his, she noticed there was a plastic wedding ring hanging from his glass, realized she had one hanging from hers, too. She laughed. "And the ring's a nice touch. The circle is the symbol of eternity."

"Again, your drink is slightly special." He sounded almost miffed, as if he was recalculating whether he should have sacrificed his trophy to Rita once again, but she couldn't seem to care.

Her heart stopped beating, she was sure of it. Time even seemed to stop. The light from the moon, the stars, the floodlights around the community center sparkled on the ring that was hanging by a loop of bright pink ribbon from the stem of her glass.

"Oh, Johnny."

He ran a hand through his abnormally neat hair. "I know it's corny, and probably way too soon, and maybe a ring doesn't prove anything, maybe getting married isn't a grand gesture, but I only had a few hours and, God, I'm nervous." He ran the back of his hand over his forehead and she thought, seeing the most relaxed man she'd ever known this worked up on her account probably told her everything she needed to know. "I memorized some things to say but I can't remember a single thing. I forget what I'm supposed to do now."

"I think you have to ask me a question," she prompted.

"Right. Good. That's it." He blew out a breath. "Will you? Will you take a chance on me? Marry me, Natalie."

"Johnny, are you sure?"

"Are you?"

"Yes." Because what other answer could there be?

He fumbled a little getting the ring free, and then slipped it onto her finger. When they kissed she tasted champagne, raspberry, and she thought she tasted the future.

She sipped her drink again.

"I'm sorry you had to sacrifice your trophy this year."

He kissed her hard.

"I already won."

* * * * *

*Drag racer and construction company owner
Beau Stillwell has his hands full trying to mess up
his sister's upcoming wedding. The guy just isn't good
enough for her. But when Beau meets Natalie Bridges,
the very determined wedding planner, he realises
he needs to change gears and do something drastic.
Like drive sexy, uptight Natalie wild…*

Turn the page for a sneak preview of

Hot-Wired
by
Jennifer LaBrecque

Hot-Wired
by
Jennifer LaBrecque

BEAU STILLWELL could kiss her ass. If she could ever find him, that was.

Her temper beginning to fray at the edges, Natalie Bridges silently huffed and carefully picked her way through yet another row of big pickup trucks, trailers, motor homes and some of the loudest, gaudiest souped-up cars she'd ever had the misfortune to see. Welcome to Dahlia Speedway, where big boys and their toys hurtled down a quarter-mile track to see who could go the fastest. Quite frankly, she didn't get it.

What, or rather who, she needed to get, however, was Beauregard Stillwell. She'd called and left messages every day for two weeks with the secretary of Stillwell Construction. He'd summarily ignored them. She'd doggedly left messages on his cell and home phone. No call back.

She jumped as a car cranked next to her with a near deafening roar. Was there another wedding planner in Nashville, Tennessee, who'd go to these lengths to get the job done? Maybe, maybe not, but she was bound and determined that Caitlyn Stillwell and Cash Vickers would have the wedding of their dreams—if she could ever get Caitlyn's brother, Beau, to cooperate.

Caitlyn and Cash had the *most* romantic story. Call it fate or destiny or karma, but fresh out of college with a degree in film and video, Caitlyn had lucked into shooting a music video for rising country music star Cash Vickers at an antebellum plantation outside Nashville. In a nutshell, they'd fallen in love with each other and the place during the filming. In a wildly romantic gesture, Cash had bought the plantation, Belle Terre, for him and Caitlyn. They both had their hearts set on getting married there. However, while a faintly neglected air worked for a video for "Homesick," a song about finding where you belong and who you belonged there with, it didn't work for a wedding. Caitlyn didn't trust anyone with the renovations except her big brother, Beau.

Which was all good and fine, if Natalie could just get him to talk to her about the renovation schedule. In the two-week span of being ignored, Natalie could've lined up another builder to handle the remodel, except this was a sticking point with Caitlyn. No Beau Stillwell, no remodel. No remodel, no wedding.

And come hell or high water, in which hell might very well take the form of Beau Stillwell, Natalie was planning and executing this wedding. Cash was being touted as country music's next big thing, and being in charge of his and Caitlyn's wedding would set Natalie apart as Nashville's premier wedding planner…but only if everything went off without a hitch. She'd either be ruined or all the rage. Ruined wasn't a viable option.

Hence, she'd finished up the rehearsal dinner for tomorrow's wedding between Gina Morris and Tommy Pitchford, settled them and their families at the private banquet room at the upscale Giancarlo's Ristorante, and left her assistant, Cynthia, to deal with any residual problems. Natalie had driven the thirty miles out of Nashville and parted with twenty dollars at the gate to gain entry to the one place she knew for sure she could find Mr. Stillwell on a Friday evening—the Dahlia drag strip.

Dodging a low-slung orange car with skulls airbrushed on the front and side as it pulled down the "street" in the congested pit area, she thought better a drag strip than a strip joint. Although she had thought it was pretty interesting the one time she'd tracked down a recalcitrant groom and dragged him out of a strip club. Her seldom-seen, inner wild girl had thought she wouldn't mind doing a pole dance for someone special in a private setting.

Even though she was about five unreturned phone calls beyond annoyed, she had to admit the drag strip was an interesting place. Apparently drag racing pit areas were wherever the car's trailer was parked. She tried to ignore the stares and titters that followed her. Maybe three-inch heels and a suit weren't the dress code at the drag strip, but changing would have meant driving all the way back across Nashville when she'd had the girl genius idea of coming here to track down Beau the Bastard, as she and Cynthia had dubbed him earlier today when he'd blown off her call yet again.

She clutched her purse tighter against her side. There was almost a carnival atmosphere. An announcer "called" the race, giving statistics and tidbits about each driver over a loudspeaker. The cars themselves were beyond loud, spectators whooped and hollered, people zoomed around on four-wheelers and golf carts, and there was plenty of tailgating going on at the race trailers. It sort of reminded her of holidays at her parents' house—chaos. Although, unlike at her folks', there was at least some structure and method behind the madness here.

She passed a concession stand located behind the packed spectator bleachers and the smell of hamburgers and French fries wafting out set her mouth watering and her stomach growling, reminding her she hadn't eaten since breakfast. God, she'd kill for a greasy fry dredged in catsup right now—the ultimate comfort food. However, she was probably packing on another five pounds just from smelling them.

She walked away from the people lined up at the burger window. Directly across from the food concession, she noticed a T-shirt vendor displayed his, or her, wares. Natalie nearly laughed aloud at the one that proclaimed "Real Men Do It With 10.5 Inches."

She didn't get the inside joke and it was rude and crude, but still kind of funny. And she had to smile at the "Damn Right It's Fast, Stupid Ass" next to it.

She was so busy laughing at the T-shirts that catching her heel in a crack caught her totally unawares. Arms flailing, she pitched into a guy…carrying a hot dog and a plastic cup of beer.

"Damn, lady," he yelled, "watch where you're going." He shot her a nasty look. "And that cost me my last eight bucks."

Natalie righted herself, dug into her purse, pulled out a ten and shoved it in the man's hand. "Sorry."

Mollified by his two-dollar gain, he changed his tune. "No problem." He looked down her chest and grimaced. "Napkins are over there." He turned on his heel and returned to the concession counter.

She glanced down. Her favorite cream silk blouse with the lovely ruffle down the center clung to her in a beer bath. Bright yellow mustard and red catsup obscured the flowers on the left breast of her jacket. She wasn't sure that blouse and jacket weren't both ruined. She quelled the urge to laugh hysterically. Napkins. She needed napkins.

She started toward the round, bar-height table that held the napkins, along with the hamburger and hot dog fixings, and realized she'd wrenched the heel off her right pump when she'd stepped in the asphalt crack. She limped over to the table and grabbed a napkin.

A blonde with dark roots in jeans and a halter top

gave her a sympathetic look. "The bathroom's right around the corner."

"Thanks."

Five minutes later, she'd managed to work some of the mustard and catsup stain out of her jacket and she'd blotted at her beer-soaked blouse. She'd toyed with, and promptly dismissed, the notion that she'd be better off trading them for one of the graphic tees. No, that would make her look even more bedraggled than her stained clothing.

For the thousandth time, she silently cursed Beau Stillwell. This was all his fault. Maybe he wasn't personally responsible for the asphalt crack she'd caught her heel in, but if he'd had the common courtesy to return just one of her phone calls or, at the very least, left a message for her with his secretary, Natalie wouldn't have been reduced to chasing him all over Dahlia, Tennessee, and her heel wouldn't have gotten stuck in the damn crack in the damn first place because she wouldn't have been here.

MILLS & BOON

Blaze

On sale 21st May 2010

(2-IN-1 ANTHOLOGY)
HOT-WIRED & COMING ON STRONG
by Jennifer LaBrecque & Tawny Weber

Hot-Wired

Beau won't let his sister marry the wrong man! But wedding planner Natalie will do *anything* – even give in to his sizzling seduction – to stop him ruining the ceremony.

Coming on Strong

Belle left Mitch at the altar six years ago but now she needs his help. Mitch is willing to give her what she needs – *if* she adheres to his seriously sensual demands first!

LETTERS FROM HOME
by Rhonda Nelson

Soldier Levi is receiving steamy anonymous letters. When he comes home, he intends to find the mystery author…and show her that actions speak louder than words!

EVERY BREATH YOU TAKE…
by Hope Tarr

FBI agent Cole never has trouble putting his life on the line… but his heart? No way. Until he is charged with guarding the one woman he's never been able to forget!

2 FREE BOOKS
AND A SURPRISE GIFT

We would like to take this opportunity to thank you for reading this Mills & Boon® book by offering you the chance to take TWO more specially selected titles from the Blaze® series absolutely FREE! We're also making this offer to introduce you to the benefits of the Mills & Boon® Book Club™—

- **FREE home delivery**
- **FREE gifts and competitions**
- **FREE monthly Newsletter**
- **Exclusive Mills & Boon Book Club offers**
- **Books available before they're in the shops**

Accepting these FREE books and gift places you under no obligation to buy, you may cancel at any time, even after receiving your free books. Simply complete your details below and return the entire page to the address below. You don't even need a stamp!

YES Please send me 2 free Blaze books and a surprise gift. I understand that unless you hear from me, I will receive 3 superb new books every month, including a 2-in-1 book priced at £4.99 and two single books priced at £3.19 each, postage and packing free. I am under no obligation to purchase any books and may cancel my subscription at any time. The free books and gift will be mine to keep in any case.

Ms/Mrs/Miss/Mr_____ Initials _____

Surname _____

Address _____

_____

_____ Postcode _____

E-mail _____

Send this whole page to: Mills & Boon Book Club, Free Book Offer, FREEPOST NAT 10298, Richmond, TW9 1BR

Offer valid in UK only and is not available to current Mills & Boon Book Club subscribers to this series. Overseas and Eire please write for details.. We reserve the right to refuse an application and applicants must be aged 18 years or over. Only one application per household. Terms and prices subject to change without notice. Offer expires 31st July 2010. As a result of this application, you may receive offers from Harlequin Mills & Boon and other carefully selected companies. If you would prefer not to share in this opportunity please write to The Data Manager, PO Box 676, Richmond, TW9 1WU.

Mills & Boon® is a registered trademark owned by Harlequin Mills & Boon Limited.
Blaze® is being used as a registered trademark owned by Harlequin Mills & Boon Limited.
The Mills & Boon® Book Club™ is being used as a trademark.